08-BVQ-362

D0020368

THE ANITA BLAKE, VAMPIRE HUNTER NOVELS

"HOT STUFF."
—*Publishers Weekly* (starred review)

✳

"HEART-POUNDING."
—*Detroit Free Press*

✳

"STEAMY."
—*Booklist*

Praise for the novels of

LAURELL K. HAMILTON
featuring Anita Blake, Vampire Hunter

"I've never read a writer with a more fertile imagination."
—*Diana Gabaldon*

"Hamilton just keeps getting better and better."
—*St. Louis Post-Dispatch*

"Anita Blake [is] the 'it' girl for bloodsuckers, were-wolves, wereleopards and assorted undead types."
—*The News-Press* (Fort Myers, FL)

"Hamilton maintains a terrific pace with suspense, revenge, and heart-pounding endings."   —*Detroit Free Press*

"Gruesome, action-packed scenes and episodes . . . The eroticism and the 'dramedy' of complicated relationships between shape-shifting lovers sets Hamilton's novels apart from the rest of the pack . . . Hamilton really does come off like the genre's answer to Henry Miller."
—*The Denver Post*

"Good, clean (or bloody) fun—meant for those who like their page-turners with a little bite to them."
—*Austin American-Statesman*

"[Anita Blake is] still the same gutsy, no-nonsense female unafraid to take on anything that the preternatural world throws her way."   —*Library Journal*

"There's plenty of life (and undeath) left in this series, and Hamilton's imagination is apparently as inexhaustible as her heroine's supernatural capacity for coupling."
—*Publishers Weekly*

"Fresh and fun."   —*Metropole*

Anita Blake, Vampire Hunter Novels by
LAURELL K. HAMILTON

Micah

Laurell K. Hamilton

JOVE BOOKS, NEW YORK

THE BERKLEY PUBLISHING GROUP
Published by the Penguin Group
Penguin Group (USA) Inc.
375 Hudson Street, New York, New York 10014, USA
Penguin Group (Canada), 90 Eglinton Avenue East, Suite 700, Toronto, Ontario M4P 2Y3,
Canada (a division of Pearson Penguin Canada Inc.)
Penguin Books Ltd., 80 Strand, London WC2R 0RL, England
Penguin Group Ireland, 25 St. Stephen's Green, Dublin 2, Ireland
(a division of Penguin Books Ltd.)
Penguin Group (Australia), 250 Camberwell Road, Camberwell, Victoria 3124, Australia
(a division of Pearson Australia Group Pty. Ltd.)
Penguin Books India Pvt. Ltd., 11 Community Centre, Panchsheel Park,
New Delhi—110 017, India
Penguin Group (NZ), Cnr. Airborne and Rosedale Roads, Albany, Auckland 1310, New
Zealand (a division of Pearson New Zealand Ltd.)
Penguin Books (South Africa) (Pty.) Ltd., 24 Sturdee Avenue, Rosebank, Johannesburg 2196,
South Africa

Penguin Books Ltd., Registered Offices: 80 Strand, London WC2R 0RL, England

This is a work of fiction. Names, characters, places, and incidents either are the product of the
author's imagination or are used fictitiously, and any resemblance to actual persons, living or
dead, business establishments, events, or locales is entirely coincidental. The publisher does not
have any control over and does not assume any responsibility for author or third-party web-
sites or their content.

MICAH

A Jove Book / published by arrangement with the author.

PRINTING HISTORY
Jove mass market edition / March 2006

Copyright © 2006 by Laurell K. Hamilton.
Excerpt from *Danse Macabre* copyright © 2006 by Laurell K. Hamilton.
Cover design by Judith Murello.
Cover illustration and stepback art by Craig White.
Text design by Kristin del Rosario.

All rights reserved.
No part of this book may be reproduced, scanned, or distributed in any printed or electronic
form without permission. Please do not participate in or encourage piracy of copyrighted ma-
terials in violation of the author's rights. Purchase only authorized editions.
For information, address: The Berkley Publishing Group,
a division of Penguin Group (USA) Inc.,
375 Hudson Street, New York, New York 10014.

ISBN: 0-515-14087-2

JOVE®
Jove Books are published by The Berkley Publishing Group,
a division of Penguin Group (USA) Inc.,
375 Hudson Street, New York, New York 10014.
JOVE is a registered trademark of Penguin Group (USA) Inc.
The "J" design is a trademark belonging to Penguin Group (USA) Inc.

PRINTED IN THE UNITED STATES OF AMERICA

10 9 8 7 6 5 4 3 2 1

If you purchased this book without a cover, you should be aware that this book is stolen prop-
erty. It was reported as "unsold and destroyed" to the publisher, and neither the author nor the
publisher has received any payment for this "stripped book."

My idea of love is
not everyone's ideal.
Some have broken
under the strain
of it. This one's for
Jon, who sees love
not as a burden,
but as a gift.

Acknowledgments

To all the people that help keep my life running smoothly: Darla Cook, Sherry Ganey, Lauretta Allen, Mary Schuermann, and Richard Nichols (no relation to the character).

To my writing group: Tom Drennan, Debbie Millitello, Rett MacPherson, Marella Sands, Sharon Shinn and Mark Summer. *Nill illigitamus carborundum.*

CHAPTER

1

It was half past dawn when the phone rang. It shattered the first dream of the night into a thousand pieces so that I couldn't even remember what the dream had been about. I woke gasping and confused, asleep just long enough to feel worse but not rested.

Nathaniel groaned beside me, mumbling, "What time is it?"

Micah's voice came from the other side of the bed, his voice low and growling, thick with sleep. "Early."

I tried to sit up, sandwiched between the two of them where I always slept, but I was trapped. Trapped in the sheets, one arm tangled in Nathaniel's hair. He usually braided it for bed, but last night we'd all gotten in late, even by our standards, and we'd just fallen into bed as soon as we could manage it.

"I'm trapped," I said, trying to extract my hand from his hair without hurting him or tangling worse. His hair was thick and fell to his ankles; there was lots of it to tangle.

"Let the machine pick up," Micah said. He'd raised up on his elbows enough to see the clock. "We've had less than an hour of sleep." His hair was a mass of tousled curls around his face and shoulders. His face was dim in the darkness of the blackout curtains.

I finally got my hand free of Nathaniel's warm, vanilla-scented hair. I lay on my side, propped on my elbow, waiting for the machine to kick in and let us know whether it was the police for me or the Furry Coalition hotline for Micah. Nathaniel, as a stripper, didn't get emergency calls much. Just as well; I wasn't sure I wanted to know what a stripper emergency call would be. The only ideas I could come up with were either silly or nefarious. Ten rings, and the machine finally kicked on. Micah spoke over the sound of his own voice on the machine's message. "Who set the machine on the second phone line to ten rings?"

"Me," Nathaniel said. "It seemed like a better idea when I did it."

We'd put in the second phone line because Micah was the main help for a hotline that new wereanimals could call and get advice or a rescue. You know, *I'm at a bar and I'm about to lose control, come get me before I turn furry in public.* It wasn't technically illegal to be a wereanimal, but new ones sometimes lost control and ate someone before they came to their senses. They'd probably be shot to death by the local police before they could be charged with murder. If the police had silver bullets. If not . . . it could get very, very bad.

Micah understood the problems of the furred, because he was the local Nimir-Raj, their leopard king.

There was a moment of breathing on the message, too fast, frantic. The sound made me sit up in bed, letting the sheets pool into my lap. "Anita, Anita, this is Larry. You there?" He sounded scared.

Nathaniel got the receiver before I did, but he said, "Hey, Larry, she's here." He handed me the receiver, his face worried.

Larry Kirkland—fellow federal marshal, animator, and vampire executioner—didn't panic that easily anymore. He'd grown, or aged, since he'd started working with me.

"Larry, what's wrong?"

"Anita, thank God." His voice held more relief than I ever wanted to hear in anyone's voice. It meant he expected me to do something important for him. Something that would take some awful pressure or problem off their hands.

"What's wrong, Larry?" I asked, and I couldn't keep the worry out of my own voice.

He swallowed hard enough for me to hear it. "I'm okay, but Tammy isn't."

I clutched the receiver. His wife was Detective Tammy Reynolds, member of the Regional Preternatural Investigation Squad. My first thought was that she'd been hurt in the line of duty. "What happened to Tammy?"

Micah leaned in against me. Nathaniel had gone very quiet beside me. We'd all been at their wedding. Hell, I'd been at the altar on Larry's side.

"The baby. Anita, she's in labor."

It should have made me feel better, but it didn't, not by much. "She's only five months pregnant, Larry."

"I know, I know. They're trying to get the labor stopped, but they don't know . . ." He didn't finish the sentence.

Tammy and Larry had been dating for a while when Tammy ended up pregnant. They'd married when she was four months pregnant. Now the baby that had made them both change all their plans might never be born. Or at least not survive. Shit.

"Larry, I'm . . . Jesus, Larry, I'm so sorry. Tell me what I can do to help." I couldn't think of anything, but whatever he asked, I'd do it. He was my friend, and there was such anguish in his voice. He'd never mastered that empty cop voice.

"I'm due on an eight a.m. flight to raise a witness for the FBI."

"The federal witness who died before he could testify," I said.

"Yeah," Larry said. "They need the animator that brings him back to be one of us who's also a federal marshal. Me being a federal marshal was one of the reasons the judge agreed to allow the zombie's testimony."

"I remember," I said, but I wasn't happy. I wouldn't turn him down or chicken out, not with Tammy in the hospital, but I hated to fly. No, I was afraid to fly. Damn it.

"I know how much you hate to fly," he said.

That made me smile, that he was trying to make me feel better when his life was about to break apart. "It's okay, Larry. I'll see if the flight has some empty seats. If not I'll get a later flight, but I'll go."

"All my files on the case are at Animators, Inc. I'd stopped by the office to get them and load up the briefcase when Tammy called. I think my briefcase is just sitting on the floor in our office. I got all the files in it. The agent in charge is . . ." And he hesitated. "I

can't remember. Oh, hell, Anita, I can't remember."
He was panicking again.

"It's okay, Larry. I'll find it. I'll call the Feds and
tell them there's been a change of cast."

"Bert's going to be pissed," Larry said. "Your rates
are almost four times what mine are for a zombie
raising."

"We can't change the price in midcontract," I said.

"No"—and he almost laughed—"but Bert is going
to be pissed that we didn't try."

I laughed, because he was right. Bert had been our
boss, but he'd been reduced to business manager because all the animators at Animators, Inc., had gotten
together and staged a palace coup. We'd offered him
business manager or nothing. He'd taken it when he
realized his income wouldn't be affected.

"I'll get the files from the office. I'll get a flight.
I'll be there. You just take care of yourself and
Tammy."

"Thanks, Anita. I don't know what I . . . I've got
to go—the doctor's here." And he was gone.

I handed the phone to Nathaniel, who placed it gently in the cradle.

"How bad is it?" Micah said.

I shrugged. "I don't know. I don't think Larry knows, not really." I started to crawl out of the covers and the nest of warmth that their bodies made.

"Where are you going?" Micah asked.

"I've got a plane to schedule and files to find."

"Are you thinking of going out of town on a plane by yourself?" Micah asked. He was sitting up, knees tucked to his chest, arms encircling them.

I looked back at him from the foot of the bed. "Yeah."

"When will you be back?"

"Tomorrow, or the day after."

"Then you need to book at least two seats on the plane."

It took me a moment to understand what he meant. I raised the dead and was a legal vampire executioner. That's what the police knew for certain. I was a federal marshal because all the vamp executioners who could pass the firearms test had been grandfathered in so that the executioners could both have more powers and be better regulated. Or that was the idea. But I was also the human servant of Jean-Claude, the master vampire of St. Louis. Through ties to Jean-Claude I'd inherited some abilities. One of those abilities was the *ardeur*. It was as if sex were food, and if I didn't eat enough I got sick.

That wasn't so bad, but I could also hurt anyone that I was metaphysically tied to. Not just hurt, but potentially drain them of life. Or the *ardeur* could simply choose someone at random to feed from. Which meant the *ardeur* raised and chose a victim. I didn't always have a lot of choice in who it chose. Ick.

So I fed from my boyfriends and a few friends. You couldn't feed off the same person all the time, because you could accidentally love him to death. Jean-Claude held the *ardeur* and had had to feed it for centuries, but my version was a little different from his, or maybe I just wasn't as good at controlling it yet. I was working on it, but my control wasn't perfect, and it would be a bad thing to lose control on an airplane full of strangers. Or in a van full of federal agents.

"What am I going to do?" I asked. "I cannot take my boyfriend on a federal case."

"You aren't going as a federal marshal, not really," Micah said. "It's your skills as an animator that they want, so say that I'm your assistant. They won't know any different."

"Why do you get to go?" Nathaniel asked. He lay back on the pillows, the sheets just barely covering his nakedness.

"Because she fed on you last," Micah said. He moved enough to touch Nathaniel's shoulder. "I can feed her more often than you can without passing out or getting sick."

"Because you're the Nimir-Raj and I'm just a regular wereleopard." There was a moment of sullenness in his voice, and then he sighed. "I don't mean to be a problem, but I've never stayed here with both of you gone."

Micah and I looked at each other and had one of those moments. We'd all been living together for about six months. But he and Nathaniel had both moved in at the same time. I'd never dated either of them alone, not really. I mean I'd gone out with them individually, and sex wasn't always a group activity, but the sleeping arrangements were.

Micah and I both had a certain need for personal time, alone time, but Nathaniel didn't. He didn't much like being alone.

"Do you want to stay at Jean-Claude's place while we're gone?" I asked.

"Will he want me there without you?" Nathaniel asked.

I knew what he meant, but . . . "Jean-Claude likes you."

"He won't mind," Micah said, "and Asher won't mind at all."

There was something about the way he said that last that made me look at him. Asher was Jean-Claude's second in command. They'd been friends, enemies, lovers, enemies, and shared a woman that they both loved for a few decades of happiness in centuries of unhappiness.

"Why'd you say it like that?" I asked.

"Asher likes men more than Jean-Claude does," Micah said.

I frowned at him. "Are you saying that he made a pass at you or Nathaniel?"

Micah laughed. "No, in fact, Asher is always very, very careful around us. Considering that we've both been naked in a bed with Asher, Jean-Claude, and you more than once, I'd say that Asher's been a perfect gentleman."

"So why the comment about Asher liking men more than Jean-Claude?" I asked.

"It's the way Asher watches Nathaniel when you aren't looking."

I looked at the other man in my bed. He appeared utterly at home half-naked in my sheets. "Does Asher bother you?"

He shook his head. "No."

"Have you noticed him looking at you the way Micah just said?"

"Yes," Nathaniel said, face still peaceful.

"And that doesn't bother you?"

He smiled. "I'm a stripper, Anita. I get a lot of people looking at me like that."

"But you don't sleep naked in a bed with them."

"I don't sleep naked in a bed with Asher either. He takes blood from me so he can fuck you. It may be sensual, but it's not about sex; it's about blood."

I frowned, trying to think my way through the tangle that had become my love life. "But Micah's implying that Asher sees you as more than food."

"I'm not implying," Micah said. "I'm stating that if Asher didn't think you and Jean-Claude would be pissed, he'd have already asked Nathaniel to be more than friends."

I stared from one to the other of them. "He would?"

They both nodded in unison, as if they'd practiced.

"And you both knew this?"

They nodded again.

"Why didn't you tell me?"

"Because you, or I, were always there to protect Nathaniel," Micah said. "Now we won't be."

I sighed.

"I'll be okay," Nathaniel said. "If I'm really that worried about my virtue, I'll bunk in with Jason." He smiled even wider.

"What's so funny?" I asked. I sounded angry, because I had totally missed the whole Asher-liking-Nathaniel thing. Sometimes I felt slow, and sometimes I felt totally unprepared for dealing with the men in my life.

"The look on your face, so worried, so surprised." He bounced up off the bed, leaving the sheet behind him. He crawled toward me, naked and beautiful. I was at the end of the bed and had nowhere to go. But he came at me so fast that I tried to back up and ended up falling off the bed. I sat naked on the floor, trying to decide if I had any dignity left to save.

Nathaniel leaned over the bed and grinned at me. "If I tell you that was really cute, will you be mad at me?"

"Yes," I said, but I was fighting not to smile.

He leaned his upper body off the bed, toward me. "Then I won't say it," he said. "I love you, Anita." He leaned down, but if we were going to kiss I'd have to come to my knees and meet him halfway.

I moved into the kiss he was offering and whispered against his lips, "I love you, too."

"Tell me what city we're flying to," Micah said from the bed, "and I'll see about flights."

I broke the kiss enough to mumble, "Philadelphia."

Nathaniel leaned in to me again, one hand holding on to the bedpost to keep him in place. The muscles of his arm flexed effortlessly as he used the other hand to smooth hair away from my face. "I'll miss you."

"I'll miss you, too," I said, and I realized that I meant it. But one "assistant" I might be able to explain to the FBI, not two. Two and they'd begin to wonder who they were and exactly what they were assisting me with. Or that's what I told myself. Staring into the startling lavender of Nathaniel's eyes, I wondered if I cared what the FBI thought of me enough to leave him behind. Almost not. Almost.

CHAPTER

2

We picked up Larry's files on the way to the airport. Micah drove so I could find a phone number to call and let everyone in Philly know that there'd been a change of cast. The business card read, *Special Agent Chester Fox.*

He answered on the second ring. "Fox." Not even a hello. What was it about police work that made you have bad phone manners?

"This is Federal Marshal Anita Blake. You're expecting Marshal Kirkland this morning?"

"He's not coming," Fox guessed.

"No, but I am."

"What happened to Kirkland?"

"His wife is in the hospital." I wondered how much I owed him on the phone. I decided not much.

"I hope she's going to be all right." His voice had lost some of its edge. He sounded almost friendly. It made me think better of him.

"She probably will, but they're not sure about the baby."

Silence for a moment. I'd probably over-shared. That girlness again. Harder to be terse.

"I didn't know. I'm sorry that Marshal Kirkland couldn't make it and even sorrier for the reason. I hope things work out for them."

"Me, too. So I'm filling in."

"I know who you are, Marshal Blake." He was back to not sounding entirely happy. "Your reputation precedes you." That last was definitely not happy.

"Are we going to have a problem here, Agent Fox?"

"Special Agent Fox," he said.

"Fine, are we going to have a problem here, Special Agent Fox?"

"Are you aware that you have the highest kill count of any legal vampire executioner in this country?"

"Yeah, actually, I am aware of that."

"You're coming here to raise the dead, Marshal, not execute anyone. Is that clear?"

Now I was getting pissed. "I don't kill people for the hell of it, Special Agent Fox."

"That's not what I've heard." His voice was quiet.

"Don't believe all the rumors you hear, Fox."

"If I believed them all, I wouldn't let you step foot in my city, Blake."

Micah touched my leg, just to be comforting, while he drove one-handed. We were already on 70, which meant we'd be at the airport in moments.

"You know, Fox, if you're this unhappy with me, we can turn around and not come. Raise your own damn zombie."

"We?"

"I'm bringing an assistant," I said, voice angry.

"And exactly what does he assist you with?" And his voice was full of that tone, that tone that men have been using against women for centuries. That tone that manages to imply we're sluts without ever saying so.

"I'm going to be very clear here, Special Agent Fox." My voice held that calm, cold anger that I used in place of screaming. Micah's hand tightened on my thigh. "Your attitude makes me think we won't be able to work together. That you've listened to so many rumors that you wouldn't know truth if it bit you on the ass."

He started to say something, but I cut him off.

"Think very carefully about the next thing you say, Special Agent Fox, because depending on what it is, I may or may not be seeing you in Philly today, or ever."

"Are you saying if I don't play nice, you won't play at all?" His voice was as cold as mine had been.

"Nice, hell. Fox, I'd just take professional at this point. What has got your panties in a twist about me?"

He sighed over the phone. "I researched the federal marshals who are also animators. It's a short list."

"Yeah," I said, "it is."

"Kirkland comes in, does the job, leaves. Every time you get involved in a case, it all seems to go to hell."

I took a deep breath and counted to twenty. Ten didn't do it. "Go back through and look at the kind of cases that I get called in on, Fox. No one calls me in unless things have already gone south. It's not cause and effect."

"You have worked some rough shit. I'll grant that, Marshal Blake." He sighed again. "But you've got a reputation for killing first and asking questions later. As for rumors, you're right—they don't paint a very flattering picture of you."

"You might bear in mind, Fox, that any man you've heard dirty stories about me from didn't get to fuck me."

"You're sure of that."

"Absolutely."

"So you're saying that it's sour grapes, because he didn't get the prize."

"So we are talking about someone specific. Who?"

He was quiet for a second or two. "You worked a serial killer case in New Mexico about two years ago. Do you remember it?"

"Anyone who worked that case will remember it, Agent Fox. Special Agent Fox. Some things you don't forget."

"Did you date anyone while you were out there?"

The question puzzled me. "You mean in New Mexico?"

"Yes."

"No, why?"

"There was a cop named Ramirez."

"I remember Detective Ramirez. He asked me out, I said no, and he didn't trash me."

"How can you be sure of that?"

"Because he was a good guy, and good guys don't trash you just because you turned them down."

Micah was idling in front of one of the parking garages on Pear Tree Lane. We'd turned off of 70, and I hadn't really noticed. "Are we parking?" he asked. What Micah was asking was, Are we going to Philadelphia?

"Did any of the agents on scene ask you out?" His voice was serious and not hostile now.

"Not that I remember."

"Did you have a problem with anyone while you were there?"

"Lots of people."

"You admit it."

"Fox, I am female, I clean up well, have a badge and a gun, raise the dead for a living, and slay vampires. A lot of people have issues with some of the above. Hell, a lieutenant in New Mexico quoted the Bible at me."

"What quote?"

" 'Thou shalt not suffer a witch to live.' "

"He did not." He sounded shocked, something you don't hear much from the FBI.

"Yeah, he did."

"What did you do?"

"I planted a big kiss right on his mouth."

He made a startled sound that could have been a laugh. "You really did?"

"It bothered him a hell of a lot more than hitting him would have, and it didn't get me dragged out in cuffs. But I'm betting the other cops who saw me do it gave him hell."

Fox was laughing now.

There were cars behind us, honking. "Anita, are we going?" Micah asked.

"My assistant wants to know if we're going to Philly today. Are we?"

Fox's voice still held that edge of laughter. "Yeah, come on down."

I said to Micah, "We're going to Philly."

Fox said, "Marshal Blake, I am going to do what I never do, and if you tell anyone I did, I'll deny it."

"What are you going to do?"

Micah pressed the big red button on the little stand-up ticket machine. He waited for our parking ticket to pop out. I'd told him to do valet. When you drag your ass in at zero-dark-thirty, valet was worth it.

"I apologize," Fox said. "I listened to someone who was there in New Mexico. His version of your run-in with the lieutenant was different from yours."

"What did he say?"

We were in the dimness of the parking garage now.

"He said you hit on a married man and got pissy when he said no."

"If you'd ever met Lieutenant Marks, you'd know that wasn't true."

"Not cute enough?"

I hesitated. "I guess physically he wasn't that bad, but looks aren't everything. Personality, good manners, sanity—all nice things to have."

Micah had pulled around the little glass building. The attendant was coming toward us. We were moments away from needing to get out of the car. "If we're going to make the flight, I gotta go."

"Why'd you turn down Detective Ramirez?" he asked.

I wasn't sure it was any of his business, but I answered. "I was dating someone back home. I didn't think it was fair to any of us to complicate things."

"Someone said you were all over him at the last crime scene."

I knew what he was referring to. "We hugged each other, Agent Fox, because after seeing what was in that house I think we both needed to touch something warm and alive. I let one man hold my hand and all the other men think I'm fucking him. God, there are times when I really hate being the only woman around this kind of shit."

I was out of the car. Micah was getting our bags from the back.

"Now that's not fair, Marshal. If I'd hugged Ramirez or let him hold my hand, there'd be rumors, too."

It stopped me for a second, and then I laughed. "Well, damn, I guess you're right."

Micah had traded the key for a little ticket stub. He popped the handles on the carry-on bags so they'd roll. I took one of them but let him take my briefcase, since I was still on the phone. The little bus was waiting for us and a few more passengers.

"I look forward to meeting you, Marshal Blake. Time I stopped listening to secondhand stories."

"Thanks, I guess."

"See you on the ground." And he was gone.

I folded the phone shut and was already going up the bus steps before the attendant tried to take my bag. It was the skirt outfit and the heels. I always had more offers to help with luggage when I was dressed like a girl.

Micah came up behind me, mostly ignored, though he was dressed up, too. We'd chosen his most conservative suit, but there's only so much you can do with a black Italian-cut designer suit. It looked like what it was: expensive.

No one would mistake him for a Fed of any kind. We'd pulled his thick, curly hair back in a tight French braid, which almost gave the illusion of short hair. He'd put on a white shirt with the suit and a conservative tie.

We settled into the back row of seats. He'd kept his sunglasses on even in the darkened parking garage, because behind those dark glasses was a pair of leopard eyes. A very bad man had forced him into animal form long enough, and often enough, that he couldn't return completely to human form. His eyes were yellow-green, chartreuse, and not human. They were beautiful in the tan of his skin, but they tended to freak people out, hence the glasses.

I wondered how the FBI would take the eyes. Did I care? No. Things had worked out with Special Agent Fox, or seemed to be working out. But someone who had been in New Mexico was trashing me. Who? Why? Did I care? Yeah, actually, I did.

CHAPTER

3

I hate to fly. I'm phobic of it, and we'll leave it at that.
I didn't bleed Micah, but I left little half-moon nail
impressions in his hand, though I didn't realize it until after we'd landed and were getting our bags from
overhead. Then I asked him, "Why didn't you tell me
I was hurting you?"

"I didn't mind."

I frowned at him, wishing I could see his eyes,
though truthfully they probably wouldn't have told
me anything.

Micah had never been a cop, but he had been at the mercy of a crazy person for a few years. He'd learned to keep his thoughts off his face, so that his old leader didn't beat those thoughts off for him. It meant that he had one of the most peaceful, empty faces I'd ever met. A patient, waiting sort of face like saints and angels should have but never seem to.

Micah didn't like pain, not the way Nathaniel did. So he should have said something about the nails digging into his skin. It bugged me that he hadn't.

We got trapped in the aisle of the plane, because everyone else had stood up and grabbed their bags, too. We had time for me to lean in against his back and ask, "Why didn't you say something?"

He leaned back, smiling down at me. "Truthfully?"

I nodded.

"It was sort of nice to be the brave one for a change."

I frowned at him. "What's that supposed to mean?"

He turned enough so he could lay a kiss, gently, on my lips. "It means that you are the bravest person I've ever met, and sometimes, just sometimes, that's hard on the men in your life."

I didn't kiss him back. For the first time ever with him, I did not respond to his touch. I was too busy frowning and trying to decide if I should be insulted.

"What, I'm too brave to be a girl? What kind of macho bullshit—" He kissed me. Not a little kiss, but as if he'd melt into me through my mouth. His hands slid up over the leather of my jacket. He pressed himself against me, so that every inch of him was pressed against every inch of me. He kissed me long enough and held me close enough that I felt when his body began to be happy to be there.

He drew back, leaving me breathless and gasping. I swallowed hard and managed a breathy, "No fair."

"I don't want to fight, Anita."

"No fair," I said again.

He laughed, that wonderful, irritating masculine sound that said just how delighted he was with the effect he could have on me. His lips were bright with the red of my lipstick. Which probably meant I looked like I was wearing clown makeup now.

I tried to scowl at him but couldn't quite manage it. It was hard to scowl when I was fighting off a stupid grin. You cannot be angry and grin at the same time. Dammit.

The line was moving. Micah started pushing his carry-on ahead of him. I liked to pull mine behind me, but he liked to push. He had the briefcase, too. He'd pointed out that as the assistant he should be carrying more. I might have argued, but he'd kissed me, and I couldn't think fast enough to argue.

Micah had had about the same effect on me from the first moment I'd met him. It had been lust at almost first sight or maybe first touch. I was still a little embarrassed about that. It wasn't like me to fall for someone so quickly, or so hard. I'd really expected it to burn out or for us to have some huge fight and end it, but six months and counting. Six months and no breakup. It was a record for me. I'd dated Jean-Claude for a couple of years, but it had been off again, on again. Most of my relationships were. Micah was the only one who had ever come into my life and managed to stay.

Part of how he managed it was that every time he touched me I just fell to pieces. Or that's what it felt like. It felt weak, and very girlie, and I didn't like it.

The flight attendant hoped I'd had a pleasant flight. She was smiling just a little too hard. How much lipstick was I wearing and on how much of my face?

The only saving grace was we could hit a bathroom and get cleaned up before we met the FBI. They could pass through security with their badges, but these days even the Feds didn't like to abuse their privileges around airport security.

I was wearing my gun in its shoulder holster but I'd been certified to carry on an airplane. Federal marshal or no, you had to go through special training these days to carry on a plane. Sigh.

I got some looks and a few giggles as I hit the main part of the airport. I sooo needed a mirror.

Micah turned, fighting not to grin. "I made a mess of your lipstick. Sorry."

"You're not sorry," I said.

"No," he said, "I'm not."

"How bad is it?"

He let go of the carry-on handle and used his thumb to wipe across my chin. His thumb came away crimson.

"Jesus, Micah."

"If you'd been wearing base, I wouldn't have done it." He lifted his thumb to his mouth and licked it, pushing way more of the thumb into his mouth than he needed to. I watched the movement sort of fascinated. "I love the taste of your lipstick."

I shook my head and looked away from him. "Stop teasing me."

"Why?"

"Because I can't work if you keep making me moon over you."

He laughed, that warm masculine sound again.

I took hold of my carry-on and strode past him. "It's not like you to tease me this much."

He caught up with me. "No, it's usually Nathaniel, or Jean-Claude, or Asher. I behave myself unless you're mad at me."

I thought about that and it made me slow. That and the three-inch heels. "Are you jealous of them?"

"Not jealous in the way you mean. But, Anita, this is the first time that you and I have ever been on our own. Just you, just me, no one else."

That stopped me, literally, so that the man behind us cursed and had to go around abruptly. I turned and looked at Micah. "We've been alone before. We've gone out just the two of us."

"But never for more than a few hours. We've never been overnight, just us."

I thought about it because it seemed like in six months we should have managed at least one night with only the two of us. I thought, and thought, until my puzzler was sore, but he was right. We had never been overnight, just us.

"Well, damn," I said.

He smiled at me, his lips still bright with my lipstick. "There's a bathroom right over there."

We pulled the suitcases over against the wall and I left Micah in a small line of men who were also watching bags and purses. Some of them had children in tow.

There was a line in the bathroom, of course, but once I made it clear I wasn't jumping the line but repairing makeup, no one got mad. In fact, a few of them speculated, good-naturedly, on what I'd been doing to get my lipstick smeared that badly.

I did look like I was wearing clown makeup. I got my little bag of makeup, which Micah had made sure I took in with me, out of the briefcase. I'd have probably forgotten it. I had very gentle eye makeup remover that worked on anything, including lipstick. I got the mess cleaned off, then reapplied lip liner and lipstick.

The lipstick was very, very red. It made my skin seem almost translucent in its paleness. My hair gleamed black in the lights, matching the deep, solid brown of my eyes. I'd added a little eye shadow and mascara at home, and called the makeup done. I rarely wore base.

Micah was right, without the base the makeup wasn't ruined, but . . . but. I was still pissed about it. Still wanted to be angry. Wanted to be angry, not was still angry. Why did I want to hold on to the anger? Why did it make me mad that he had the ability to drown my anger with the touch of his body? Why did that bug me so much?

Because it was me. I had a real talent for picking my love life apart until I broke it. I had promised myself, not that long ago, that I'd stop picking at things. That if my life worked, I'd just enjoy it. It sounded so simple, but it wasn't. Why is it that the simplest plans are sometimes the hardest to do?

I took a deep breath and paused at the full-length mirror on the way out. I would have worn black but Bert always thought that that gave the wrong impression. Too funereal, he'd say. My silk shell was the red of the lipstick, but Bert had already complained months ago: no more black and red—too aggressive. So I was in charcoal gray with a thin pattern of black and darker gray through it. The jacket hit me at the waist to meet up with the matching skirt.

The skirt was pleated, forming a nice swing around my upper thighs when I moved. I'd tested it at home, but now I tested it again, just in case. Nope, not a glimpse of the top of my stockings. I didn't own any panty hose anymore. I'd finally been won over to the truth that a comfortable garter belt, hard to find but worth the search, with a pair of nice hose was actually more comfortable than panty hose. You just had to make sure that no one caught a glimpse of them when you moved, unless you were on a date. Men reacted really oddly if they knew you were wearing stockings and a garter belt.

If I'd known that Agent Fox had already been prejudiced against me, I might have worn a pantsuit. Too late now. Why was it a crime for a woman to look good?

Would I get fewer rumors if I dressed down? Maybe. Of course, if I wore jeans and a T-shirt I got complaints that I was too casual and needed to look more professional. Sometimes you just can't win for losing.

I was delaying. Dammit. I did not want to go back out to Micah. Why? Because he was right, this was the first time we'd ever been alone together for this long.

Why did that thought tighten my chest and make my pulse speed like something alive in my throat?

I was scared. Scared of what? Scared of Micah? Sort of. But more scared of myself, I think. Scared that without Nathaniel, or Jean-Claude, or Asher, or someone to balance things, Micah and I wouldn't work. That without everyone interfering, there wouldn't be a relationship. That there would be too much time, too much truth, and it would all fall apart. I didn't want it to fall apart. I didn't want Micah to go away. And the moment you care that much, a man has you. He owns a little piece of your soul, and he can beat you to death with it.

Don't believe me? Then you've never been in love and had it go to hell. Lucky you.

I took a deep calming breath and let it out slow. I used some of the breathing exercises I'd been studying. I was trying to learn to meditate. So far I was good at the breathing part, but I just couldn't still my mind, not without it filling with ugly thoughts, ugly images. Too much violence inside my head. Too much violence in my life. Micah was one of my refuges. His arms, his body, his smile. His quiet acceptance of me, violence and all. Now I was back to being scared. Shit.

I took another deep breath and walked out of the bathroom. I couldn't hide in there all day; the Feds were waiting. Besides, you can't hide from yourself. Can't hide from your own head going ugly. Unfortunately.

Micah smiled when he saw me. That smile that was just for me. That smile that seemed to loosen something tight and hard and bitter inside me. When he smiled at me like that, I could breathe better. So stupid, so stupid, to let anyone mean that much to you.

Something must have shown on my face because the smile dimmed around the edges. He held his hand out to me.

I went to him but didn't take his hand because I knew the moment I did I wouldn't be able to think as clearly.

He let his hand fall. "What's wrong?" The smile was gone, and it was my fault. But I'd learned to talk about my paranoias. Otherwise they grew.

I stepped closer and dropped my voice as much as the murmurous noise of the airport would allow. "I'm scared."

He moved closer to me, lowering his head. "Of what?"

"Being alone with you."

He smiled and started to reach for me. I didn't step away. I let his hands touch my arms. He held me and searched my face as if looking for a clue. I don't think he found one. He drew me into a hug and said, "Honey, if I'd dreamed that you'd be spooked about being alone with me, I wouldn't have said it."

I clung to him, my cheek pressed into his shoulder. "It would have still been true."

"Yes, but if I hadn't pointed it out, you probably wouldn't have thought about it." He held me close. "We'd have had our time away and it would never have occurred to you that it was the first time. I'm sorry."

I wrapped my hands tighter around the solidness of him. "I'm sorry, Micah. Sorry I'm such a mess."

He drew me away enough so he could gaze into my face. "You are not a mess."

I gave him a look.

He laughed and said, "Maybe a little messy, but not a mess." His voice had gone all gentle. I loved his voice like that, loved that I was the only one his voice went soft for. So why couldn't I just enjoy him, us? Hell if I knew.

"The Feds are waiting for us," I said.

It was his turn to give me a look. Even with the dark glasses, I knew the look.

"I'll be okay," I said. I gave him a smile that almost worked. "I promise to try to enjoy the parts of this trip that are enjoyable. I promise to try to not get in my own way, or weird myself out about us being . . . just us." I shrugged when I said the last.

He touched the side of my face. "When will you stop panicking about being in love?"

I shrugged again. "Never, soon, I don't know."

"I'm not going anywhere, Anita. I like it right here, beside you."

"Why?" I asked.

"Why what?"

"Why do you love me?"

He looked startled. "You mean that, don't you?"

I realized I did. I had one of those *aha* moments. I didn't think I was very lovable, so why did he love me? Why did anyone love me?

I touched his lips with my fingers. "Don't answer now. We don't have time for deep therapy. Business now. We'll work on my neuroses later."

He started to say something but I shook my head.

"Let's go meet Special Agent Fox." When I took my hand away from his lips, he just nodded. One of the reasons we worked as a couple was that Micah knew when to let it go, whatever the "it" of the moment happened to be.

This was one of those times when I truly didn't know why he put up with me. Why anyone put up with me. I didn't want to ruin this. I didn't want to pick at Micah and me until we unraveled. I wanted to leave it alone and enjoy it. I just didn't know how to do that.

We got our bags settled, and off we went. We had FBI to meet and a zombie to raise. Raising the dead was easy; love was hard.

CHAPTER

We met the Feds at the baggage return area, as arranged. How did we know who the FBI agents were in the crowd of people, most of the men dressed in suits?

They looked like agents. I don't know what it is about FBI training but Feds always just seem to look like what they are. All flavors of cops tend to look like cops, but only FBI looks like FBI and not plain cops. Don't know what they do to them down in Quantico, but whatever it is, it sticks.

Special Agent Chester Fox, agent in charge, was very Native American. The short hair, the suit, the perfect fitting-in couldn't hide the fact that he was so very not like the rest of them. I understood now some of his pissiness on the phone. He was the first Native American agent that I'd ever found involved in a case that had nothing to do with Native Americans. If you happened to be Native American, you could usually look forward to a career of dealing with cases that called for your ethnicity but not necessarily your talents. Cases involving Native American issues were also not usually career makers, though they could be career breakers. Another interesting thing about the FBI and its dealing with Native Americans was that if you looked Indian enough, they would assign you even if the case involved a totally different tribe, with a totally different language and customs. You're Indian, right? Aren't all Indians the same?

No. But then the American government—whatever branch—has never really grasped the concept of tribal identity.

The agent with him, I knew. Agent Franklin was

tall, slender with skin dark enough to actually be black. His hair was cut shorter and closer to his head than the last time I'd seen him in New Mexico, but his hands were still graceful and nervous. He smoothed those poet's hands down his overcoat. He caught me looking and stopped that nervous dance. He offered me a hand just as if he hadn't called me a slut to his partner.

I took his hand. No hard feelings here. I even smiled though I knew it didn't reach my eyes. Franklin didn't even try to look pleased to see me. He wasn't rude, but he didn't pretend he was happy either.

"Agent Franklin, I'm surprised to see you here."

He took back his hand. "Didn't your friend Bradford tell you I'd been reassigned?" He said *friend* like he meant more, and the rest was bitter. Not obvious bitter, but it had that feel to it. Nothing he said was rude enough to start a fight, but it was close.

Special Agent Bradley Bradford was head of the FBI's Special Research section, which dealt with preternatural serial killers, or crimes involving the preternatural.

There'd been a lot of controversy about splitting those crimes out of the Investigative Support unit, the one that usually handled serial killers. At short acquaintance, Franklin had made his feelings clear on the situation. He'd been against it.

Since Bradford was his boss at the time, that had been a problem. Apparently, Franklin had been reassigned, a nonvoluntary reassignment. Not good for a career in the FBI. I was taking fallout for a political squabble that I'd had nothing to do with. Great, just great.

I started to introduce Micah, but Fox beat me to it. "Callahan, Micah Callahan." Fox was already offering his hand and smiling, way more broadly than he'd smiled for me. How did an FBI agent know Micah? "You look good."

Micah smiled not quite as broadly, like he wasn't as happy to see Agent Fox. What the hell was going on?

"Fox, I . . ." Micah tried again. "The last time you saw me, I was still in the hospital. I must have looked like shit, so I guess anything's an improvement." I could hear the uncertainty in his voice, though I doubted anyone else could. You had to know him really well to hear that note in his voice.

"Someone who came that close to dying is allowed to look like shit," Fox said.

I knew then that this probably had something to do with the attack that had made Micah a wereleopard. All I knew about it for certain was that it had been violent. Once someone uses the words *violent* and *attack,* you don't press for details. I'd figured he'd tell me more when he was ready.

Micah turned to me. His face was having trouble deciding what to do, and I was betting he was glad that the glasses hid his eyes. "Special Agent Fox was one of the agents who questioned me after my attack."

I hadn't known that his mauling had gotten federal attention. I couldn't think why it would have but I couldn't ask that here and now because it would be admitting too much ignorance. Also, I wasn't sure how much Micah wanted to share in the airport with people walking around us.

I covered. I can do blank pleasant cop face with the best of them. I did it now. "What are the odds that he'd be the agent in charge of this case?" I said, smiling, as if I knew exactly what we were talking about. I'd give Micah a chance to explain later, when we didn't have an audience.

"I didn't know that you were an animator," Fox said, still talking to Micah.

"I'm not." And Micah left it at that.

Fox waited for him to add more, but Micah smiled and didn't. Fox would have let it go, but Franklin didn't. Some people just can't leave well enough alone.

"Are you a vampire executioner?" Franklin asked.

Micah shook his head.

"You're not a federal marshal." And Franklin said it like he was positive.

"No, I'm not."

"Let it go, Franklin," Fox said.

"She's brought a civilian along on a federal case."

"We'll talk about this in the car," Fox said, and the look he gave Franklin stopped the taller man in midsentence.

Fox asked me, "Do we need to wait for more bags?"

"No," I said. "We're going back home tomorrow, right?"

"That's the plan," he said, but his face was not happy, as if the whole thing with Franklin was still bothering him.

"Then we're ready to go."

He actually smiled. "A woman who packs light— that's rare."

"Sexist," I said.

He gave me a nod. "Sorry, you're right. I apologize."

I smiled and shook my head. "No sweat."

He led the way out the doors, and there were two cars waiting. One had two other agents with it, and the other was empty and waiting for us.

Fox spoke over his shoulder at us. "With the new regulations, even the FBI doesn't get to leave cars parked unattended."

"Glad to hear the new rules apply to everyone," I said, more for something to say than because I cared. I wanted to look at Micah and was afraid to. Afraid if I gave him too much attention, he'd fall apart or feel like he had to explain in front of them. Of course, by not looking at him, he might think I was mad about him not sharing details. But . . . oh, hell.

We were pretending he was just my assistant. Holding his hand or giving him a kiss might expose that lie. Or give Franklin even more reason to think I was sleeping around. I hadn't thought about what it might mean to introduce Micah as my assistant. I guess I hadn't really thought it through at all. In my own defense, I hadn't had time to come up with a good explanation for why I needed to bring my boyfriend along. *Assistant* had seemed like a good idea at the time.

I did the only thing I could think of to reassure him and keep the assistant thing going: I patted him on the shoulder. It wasn't much, but he rewarded me with a smile, as if he'd known the mental gymnastics I was going through. Maybe he did.

Fox drove. Franklin rode shotgun. Micah, the briefcase, and I rode in the backseat. The other car followed us as we pulled away.

"We'll drop you at the motel," Fox began.

Micah interrupted him. "Actually, I booked us into the Four Seasons."

"Jesus," Franklin said.

"The FBI won't pick up the tab for the Four Seasons," Fox said.

"We wouldn't expect it," Micah said.

I sat there wondering why Micah had changed hotels, then realized that Fox had said *motel*. Oh. Micah wanted a nicer place for our first night alone together. Logical—so why did it make my stomach tight? What was he expecting of our first night alone?

"Are you really going to let her bring a civilian into our case?"

Fox looked at Franklin. Even from the backseat it didn't look friendly. "I suggest, strongly, that you let this go, Agent Franklin."

"Jesus, what is it about her?" Franklin said. "She blinks those big brown eyes and everyone just looks the other way while she breaks a dozen rules and bends the very law we're sworn to uphold." He turned around in the seat as far as the seat belt would let him. "How do you do it?"

Fox said, "Franklin," and the word was a warning.

"No, Fox, it's all right. If we don't get this settled, Agent Franklin and I won't be able to work together, will we, Agent Franklin?" My voice wasn't friendly when I said all that. "You want to know how I do it?"

"Yeah," Franklin said, "I do."

"I know how you think I do it. You think I fuck everyone. But I've never met Fox, so that can't be it. So now you're scrambling, trying to figure it out."

He scowled at me.

"When you thought it was just sex, just a woman sleeping her way through her career, you were sort of okay with it, but now, now you just don't get it."

"No," he said, "I don't. Fox is the most by-the-book agent I've ever worked with, and he's letting you cart around a civilian. That's not like him."

"I know the civilian," Fox said. "That makes a difference."

"He was a victim of a violent crime. So what? You knew him how long ago?"

"Nine years," Fox said in a soft voice, his dark eyes on the traffic, hands careful on the wheel.

"You don't know what kind of person he is now. Nine years is a long time. He must have been a teenager then."

"He was eighteen," Fox's careful voice said.

"You don't know him now. He could be a bad guy for all you know."

Fox glanced in the rearview mirror. "You a bad guy, Micah?"

"No, sir," Micah said.

"That's it?" Franklin said, and he looked like he was going to work himself into hysterics or a stroke. "You ask if he's a bad guy, and he says no, and that's good enough?"

"I saw what he survived; you didn't. He answered my questions when his voice was only a hoarse rasp because the killer had clawed out his throat. I worked for Investigative Support for five years and what was done to him is still one of the worst things I've ever seen." He had to slam on the brakes to keep from hitting the sudden line of traffic in front of us. We all got very well acquainted with our seat belts, and then he continued. "He doesn't have to prove anything to you, Franklin, and he's already proven anything he ever needed to prove to me. You are going to lay off him and Marshal Blake."

"But don't you even want to know why he's here? What she brought him for? It's an ongoing case. He could be a reporter for all you know."

Fox let out a long, loud breath. "I'll let them answer this question once, just once, and then you let it go, Franklin. Let it go before I start having more sympathy with why Bradford had you reassigned."

That stopped Franklin for a second or two. The traffic started creeping forward. We seemed to be caught in rush-hour traffic. I thought at first that the threat would make him give it up but Franklin was made of sterner stuff than that.

"If he's not an animator or a vampire executioner, then what does he assist you with, Marshal Blake?" He almost managed to keep the sarcasm out of the "Marshal Blake."

I was tired of Franklin, and I'm not that good at lying. I'd had less than two hours of sleep and had to fly on a plane. So I told the truth, the absolute truth.

"When you need to have sex three, four times a day, it's just more convenient to bring your lover with you, don't you think, Agent Franklin?" I gave him wide, innocent eyes.

He gave me a sour look. Fox laughed.

"Very funny," Franklin said, but he settled back in his seat and he left us alone. The truth may not set you free, but used carefully, it can confuse the hell out of your enemies.

CHAPTER

5

The hotel was nice. Very nice. Too nice. There were people in uniforms all over the place. Not police—hotel employees. They sprang forward to get doors. To try to help with luggage. Micah actually let a bellman take our bags. I protested that we could carry them. He'd smiled and said to just enjoy it. I hadn't enjoyed it. I had leaned against the mirrored wall of the elevator and tried not to get angry.

Why was I angry? The hotel had surprised me, badly. I'd come expecting a clean-but-nothing-special room. Now we were going up in a glass and gilt elevator with a guy in white gloves pressing the buttons, explaining how the security on our little key cards worked.

My stomach was a tight knot. I had crossed my arms under my breasts, and even to me, I looked angry in the shiny mirrors.

Micah leaned beside me but didn't try to touch me. "What's wrong?" he asked, voice mild.

"I didn't expect this kind of . . . place."

"You're mad because I booked us into a nice hotel with a nice room?"

Put that way, it sounded stupid. "No, I mean . . ." I closed my eyes and leaned my head back against the glass. "Yes," I finally said, voice soft.

"Why?" he asked.

The elevator doors opened and the bellman smiled and stood so he held the doors open but left us plenty of room to move past him. If he'd figured out we were fighting, it didn't show.

Micah waved me in front of him. I pushed away from the elevator wall and went. The hallway was what I'd expected from the rest of the hotel; all dark, expensive wallpaper with curved candlelike lights at just the right intervals, so it was both well-lit and strangely intimate. There were real paintings on the wall, not copies. No big-name artists but real art. I'd never been in a hotel so expensive.

I ended up in front with Micah close behind and the bellman bringing up the rear. I realized halfway down the dark, thick carpeting that I didn't know what room I was looking for. I looked back at the bellman and said, "Since I don't know where I'm going, should I be in front?"

He smiled, as if I'd said something clever. He walked faster without seeming to hurry. He took the lead and we followed him. Which made more sense to me.

Micah walked beside me. He still had the briefcase over one shoulder. He didn't try to hold my hand; he just put his hand down where I could grab it if I wanted to. We walked like that for a few steps. His hand waiting for mine, my arms crossed.

Why was I mad? Because he'd surprised me with a really nice hotel room. What a bastard. He hadn't done anything wrong, except make me even more nervous about what he expected from me on this trip. That wasn't his bad, it was mine. My issue, not his. He was behaving like a normal civilized human being. I was being churlish and ungrateful. Dammit.

I unwound my arms. They were actually stiff with anger and holding so tight. Shit. I took his hand without looking at him. He wrapped his fingers around mine and just that little bit of touch made my stomach feel better. It would be all right. I was living with him, for God's sake. He was already my lover. This wouldn't change anything. The tight feeling in my chest didn't get better, but it was the best I could do.

The hotel room had a living room. A real living room with a couch, a marble-topped coffee table, a comfy chair with its own reading lamp, and a table in front of the far picture window that was big enough to seat four. And there were enough chairs to do that. All the wood was real and polished to a high shine. The upholstery matched but not exactly, so that it looked like a room that had grown together piece by piece instead of being bought all at once. The bathroom was full of marble-and-gleaming everything. The tub was smaller than the one we had at home, let alone Jean-Claude's tub at his club, the Circus of the Damned, but other than that, it was a pretty good bathroom. Better than any I'd ever seen in a hotel before.

The bellman was gone when I wandered out of the bathroom. Micah was putting his wallet back in that little pocket that good suit jackets have for wallets, if your wallet is long enough and slender enough not to break the line of the suit. The wallet had been a gift from me, at Jean-Claude's suggestion.

"Whose credit card did you put this on?" I asked.

"Mine," he said.

I shook my head. "How much are you blowing on this room?"

He shrugged and smiled, reaching for the bag with the clothes in it. "It's not polite to ask how much a gift cost, Anita."

I frowned at him as he moved past me to a pair of huge French doors on the far wall. "I guess I didn't think of this as a gift."

He pushed one side of the doors inward and moved through it, talking over his shoulder. "I was hoping you'd like the room."

I trailed behind him but stopped in the doorway. The bedroom had two dressers, an entertainment center, two bedside tables with full-size lamps, and a king-size bed. The bed was piled high with pillows, and everything was white and gilt and tastefully elegant. And way too bridal suite for me.

Micah had the suiter in the lid of the carry-on unrolled. He unhooked the hangers from the loops and turned to the large closet.

"This place is bigger than my first apartment," I said. I was still leaning against the folded door, not quite in the room. As if, by keeping one foot in the other room, I'd be safer.

Micah still had his sunglasses on as he unpacked us. He hung up the other suits we'd bought so they wouldn't wrinkle. Then he turned to me. He looked at me, shaking his head. "You should see the look on your face."

"What?" I asked, and even to me it sounded grumpy.

"I'm not going to make you do anything you don't want to do, Anita." He sounded less than pleased. Micah seldom got upset about anything, and almost never with me. I liked that about him.

"I'm sorry this is weirding me out."

"Do you have any idea why it's bothering you this much?" He took off the glasses and his face looked finished, with his eyes showing. The kitty-cat eyes had bothered me a little at first, but now they were just Micah's eyes. They were an amazing mix of yellow and green. If he wore green, they looked almost perfectly green. If he wore yellow—well, you get the idea.

He smiled, and it was the smile he used only at the house. Only for me and Nathaniel, or maybe just for me. At that moment, it was just for me.

"Now, that is a much better look."

"What?" I said again, but couldn't keep the smile off my face or out of my voice. Hard to be sullen when you're staring at someone's eyes and thinking how beautiful they are.

He walked toward me, and just that—him walking across the room toward me—sped my pulse, made my breath catch in my throat. I wanted to run to him, to press our bodies together, to lose the clothes and what was left of my inhibitions. But I didn't run to him because I was afraid to. Afraid of how much I wanted him, of how much he meant to me. That scared me, a lot.

He stopped in front of me, not touching me, just looking at me. He was the only man in my life who didn't have to look down to meet my eyes. In my heels, I was actually a little taller.

"God, your face! Hopeful, eager, and afraid, all there on your face." He laid his hand against my cheek. He was so warm, so warm. I curved my face into his hand and let him hold me.

"So warm," I whispered.

"I'd have had flowers waiting, but since Jean-Claude sends you roses every week, there didn't seem to be a reason for me to send you flowers."

I drew back from him, searching his face. It was peaceful, the way it could be when he was hiding his feelings. "Are you mad about the flowers?"

He shook his head. "That'd be silly, Anita. I knew I wasn't the top of your dating food chain when I hit town."

"So why bring up the flowers?" I asked.

He let out a long breath. "I didn't think it bothered me, but maybe it does. A dozen white roses every week, with a red rose added since you started having sex with Jean-Claude. And now there are two more red roses in the bouquet; one for Asher and one for Richard. So it's like the flowers are from all three of them."

"Richard wouldn't see it that way," I said.

"No, but he's still one of your lovers, and you still get something every week that reminds you of him." He frowned, shook his head. "This room is my flowers to you, Anita. Why won't you let me give it to you?"

"The flowers are a lot less expensive than this room," I said.

He frowned harder and it wasn't a look I'd seen much on his face. "Is it money that makes the difference for you, Anita? I draw a decent salary from chairing the Furry Coalition."

"You've earned the salary, Micah. You average, what, sixty hours a week?"

"I'm not saying I don't deserve the money, Anita. I'm just asking why you won't take this from me, when you take gifts from Jean-Claude?"

"I didn't like the flowers at first either. You got to town just after I'd given up fighting about it with him."

He smiled then, but it wasn't a really happy smile. More rueful. "We're going home tomorrow, Anita. I don't have time for you to get used to the idea." He sighed. "I was looking forward to spending some time, just us, and you aren't happy about it. I think my feelings are hurt."

"I don't want to hurt your feelings, Micah." I really didn't. I touched his arm, but he stepped out of reach and went back to unpacking. The tight feeling in my stomach returned, but for a different reason.

Micah never fought with me. He never pushed about our relationship. Up until that moment, I'd have thought he was happy. But this didn't feel happy. Was that my fault because I wasn't enjoying the room? Or was this a talk that had been coming, and I just hadn't known it?

"You know," he said from the bed, "you are the only woman I know who wouldn't be asking me questions about how I met Agent Fox."

The change of topic was too fast for me. "What? I mean, do you want me to ask?"

He stopped with the toiletries kit in his hands, as if he had to think about his answer and moving would have interfered with the thinking. "Maybe not, but I want you to want to ask. Does that make any sense?"

I swallowed past my rapidly speeding pulse. This felt like the beginnings of a fight. I didn't want to fight, but without Nathaniel or someone else to help me talk my way out of it, I wasn't sure I knew how to derail it. "I'm not sure I understand, Micah. You don't want me to ask, but you want me to want to ask." I shook my head. "I don't understand."

"How can you, when even I don't understand it?" He looked angry for a moment, and then his face smoothed out to its usual handsome, pleasant neutrality. It had only been in the last month that I'd realized how much pain and confusion he hid behind that face. "I want you to care enough about me to be curious, Anita."

"I do care," I said, but I kept myself pressed against the open French door. My hands were behind my back, fingers clutching the door like it was an anchor to keep me from getting swept away in the emotional turmoil.

I puzzled for a way out of the fight that was coming and finally had an idea. "I thought you'd tell me when you were ready. You've never asked me about my scars." There. That was a valid point.

He smiled, and it was his old smile, the one I'd almost broken him of. The smile was sad, wistful, self-loathing, and had nothing to do with anything pleasant. It was a smile only because his lips went up instead of down.

"I guess I haven't asked about the scars. I figured you'd tell me if you wanted me to know." He had all the clothes put away, only the toiletries case still waiting on the bed. "I promised Nathaniel I'd order food when we got here," he said.

Again the conversational switch was too fast for me. "Are we changing the topic?"

He nodded. "You scored a point." He said, "You didn't like the room, and it hurt my feelings. Then you didn't seem to care about meeting Fox and hearing more details about my attack. I thought, if she cared, she'd want to know more."

"So we're not going to fight?"

"You're right, Anita, I've never asked how you got any of your scars. I've never asked you, just like you've never asked me. I can't get angry with you for something I've done myself."

The tightness in my chest eased a little. "You'd be amazed by the number of people who would still fight about it."

He smiled, still not happy, but a little better. "But I would really like it if you'd try to enjoy the room and not act like I've lured you here for nefarious purposes."

I took a deep breath and let it out, then nodded. "It's a beautiful room, Micah."

He smiled, and this time it reached his kitty-cat eyes. "Just like that, you'll try."

I nodded. "If it means that much to you, yes."

He took a deep breath, as if his own chest had been a little tight. "I'll put the toiletries up, then look at the room service menu."

"Nathaniel was pretty put out that he didn't get to make us a real breakfast," I said, still clinging to the door.

"I remember when a bagel was breakfast," Micah said.

"Hell," I said, "I remember when coffee was breakfast."

"I don't," he said. "I've been a lycanthrope too long. We have to eat regularly to help control our beasts."

"One hunger feeds the other," I said.

"I'll order food. You look at the file."

"I looked at it on the plane."

"Do you remember anything you read?"

I thought about it, then shook my head. "No. I'd hoped it would help take my mind off of the whole being hundreds of feet above the ground situation, but I guess it didn't really help."

"I noticed just how unhelpful it was." He raised his hand up. There were still dim marks of my nails. Considering how fast he healed, that meant I'd actually hurt him.

"Jesus, Micah, I'm sorry."

He shook his head. "I'm not complaining. Like I said on the plane, it was interesting to see you so . . . so shaken."

"You being there helped," I said in a small voice.

"Glad to hear that I spilled blood for a good cause."

"Did I really bleed you?"

He nodded. "It's healed, but yeah, you did. You still aren't quite used to being more than human strong."

"I'll read the file because I need to before tonight, but if you want to tell me about how you became a wereleopard, you can. Honestly, once you told me it was an attack, I treated you like any survivor. You don't question survivors about the trauma; you let them come to you."

He walked toward the doors, and for a moment I thought he'd walk by without touching me. Which would have been bad. He gave me a quick kiss and a smile, then moved past me to put the toiletries kit in the bathroom.

I stood there for a moment, leaning against the door. We were doing the exact thing I'd feared we'd do alone together. We were raking emotional shit. I sighed and moved into the living room. The briefcase was waiting beside the couch. I got the file out and took it to the four-seater table by the big picture window. The main road was just outside, but it wound around a sidewalk that wound around a large fountain. It somehow made it seem less of a road and more of a view.

I could hear Micah puttering in the bathroom. He had to be putting out the toothbrushes, deodorant, etc. . . . I would have stopped unpacking once the good clothes were hung up. Both Micah and Nathaniel were neater and more domestically organized than I was. So was Jean-Claude I guess. I wasn't sure about Asher. But I was definitely the slob of the group.

I opened the file and started to read. There wasn't much there. The deceased's name had been Emmett Leroy Rose. He'd had a double degree from the University of Pennsylvania in accounting and prelaw. He'd gotten his law degree at the University of Pittsburgh School of Law. He'd died of a heart attack at the age of fifty-three, while in federal custody waiting to testify at an important trial. He'd been dead less than three months. It listed his race as African American, which wasn't important to me. His religion was listed as Protestant, and that information I did need. There were a few religious persuasions that could interfere with zombie raising. Vaudan—voodoo—was the big one. It could be tricky to raise someone who messed with some of the same magic that I would be using. Wiccan could also make things difficult, and so could some of the more mystically oriented faiths. Straight Christian of whatever flavor wasn't a problem. And psychic abilities could mess with a zombie and make it either hard to raise or hard to control once you raised it. If there was anything less than normal human about Emmett Leroy Rose, it wasn't in the file.

In fact, there were some important things missing from the file. Like what had he been arrested for—what illegal activity did they catch him at that was bad enough to get him in federal custody awaiting his testimony? And exactly what did an important trial mean? Was it mob business? Was it government business? Was it something else I couldn't even think of? Who did Mr. Rose have dirt on, and what had the Feds had on him that made him willing to shovel it? Did I need to know any of the above to raise him from the grave? No. But I wasn't used to going into this blind. If they'd sent me this file, I'd have told them no dice without more info. Yeah, they'd have replied it was a need-to-know basis, and I'd have said if they wanted me to raise the zombie, I needed to know. Larry had just taken the crumbs they gave him and not complained.

I wondered how Tammy was doing. Did I call and

ask? Later, I decided. I'd try to get some more info out of Fox first. Truthfully, I'd had about as much emotional angst as I could deal with for a little bit. If the news was bad it would wait, and I wouldn't know what to say anyway. I said a quick prayer that Tammy and the baby would be all right. That was the most concrete thing I could do.

I called the number I had for Fox. No emotional problems, just business. What a relief.

"You have everything in the file that you need to raise Rose from the dead, Marshal Blake," Fox said.

I'd figured he'd say that, but . . . "Just tell me this. Fox, how hot was Emmett Leroy Rose?"

"What do you mean, 'hot'?" he asked, but his tone said he knew.

"How important a witness was he?"

"He died of natural causes, Blake. He wasn't murdered. There wasn't a contract out on him. We just caught him doing something bad. So bad, he didn't want to go to jail over it. So he gave us more important people. Or was going to."

"Did he have a bad heart?"

"No, if he had, we'd have had a court reporter in to take down his testimony, just in case. We found out later that his father had died of an unexpected heart attack at almost the same age."

"You see, Fox, if you'd known that, you might have gotten his testimony down sooner, right?"

He was quiet a second, then said, "Maybe."

"Is anything you haven't included in this file going to bite me on the ass later? Like a father who died of a sudden heart attack."

He made a sound that might have been a laugh. "It's a good point, Marshal Blake, but no, there's nothing we left out that will impact you or your work."

"Have you ever seen someone raise the dead, Special Agent Fox?"

He was quiet again. Then, "Yes." Just that one word.

I waited for him to say more, but he didn't. "So you're happy with the information I've got."

"Yes," he said again, and there was a tone that said this conversation was about over. "Why do I think that if I'd called you in first instead of Kirkland, you'd have been a much bigger pain in the ass?"

That made me laugh. "Oh, yes," I said. "I'm a much bigger pain in the ass than Larry."

"How's his wife doing?"

"I'm going to call them when I get off the phone with you."

"Give him my best." He hung up.

I sighed and hung up my end. Then I went for my cell phone in the front of the briefcase. I turned it on, and there was a message. I pushed buttons until the phone gave up the message. Larry's voice: "Anita, it's Larry. They've got the labor stopped. They're going to keep her overnight, just to be safe, but it looks good. Thanks for taking the run to Philadelphia. Thanks for everything." Then he laughed. "How do you like the file? Real informative, isn't it?" He laughed again, then hung up.

I sat down on the couch sort of suddenly. I don't think I'd realized how worried I was until it was all right. I didn't even like Tammy much, but Larry was my friend and it would have broken his heart.

Micah was standing in front of me. I looked up. "Tammy and the baby are going to be fine. He must have called while we were in the air."

Micah smiled and touched my face. "You're pale. You were really worried about it, weren't you?"

I nodded.

"Were you hiding it from me or didn't you know either?"

I gave him a smile that was a bit too wry to be happy. "Stop knowing me so well, dammit."

"Better than you know yourself, sometimes," he said softly. And that was a little too close to the truth.

CHAPTER

6

Room service came with a knock and a polite voice. Micah got to the door before I did, but he didn't just open it. Some people in my life I've had to teach caution to, but Micah had come with it as part of the standard boyfriend package.

He checked the peephole, then looked at me. "Room service." But he didn't open the door. I watched him take a very deep breath, scenting the air. "Smells like room service."

My hand eased back from the gun under my arm. I hadn't even realized my hand was on it until that moment. His scenting at the door had made me think, just for a second, that something was wrong, not that he was simply scenting the air because it smelled good.

He put his sunglasses on before he opened the door. I made sure my jacket was covering the gun. Didn't want to weird anyone out, and definitely didn't want to give the staff a reason to talk. Hiding how far outside normal we were was standard practice. People tend to get nervous around guns and shapeshifters. Go figure.

The guy smiled and asked where we'd like the tray set up. We let him put a cloth on the table by the window.

It seemed to take a long time for him to get everything ready. He placed water glasses, real napkins, even a rose in a vase in the center of the table. I'd never seen anything this elaborate from room service.

Finally, he was done. Micah signed for the food, and the guy left with a *Have a nice day* that actually sounded sincere.

Micah shut the door behind him, putting all the locks in place. I approved. Locks don't help you if you don't use them.

I was trying to decide whether to frown. "I like the caution—you know I do."

"But," he said, setting the sunglasses on the coffee table.

"But I thought I should compliment you before I complain about something else."

His smile slipped a little. "What now?"

"There's a salad here with grilled chicken on it and a butterflied chicken breast grilled with veggies. The salad better not be mine."

He grinned then, and it was that sudden grin that gave me a glimpse of what he might have looked like at fifteen.

"You get the chicken breast."

I frowned. "I would have preferred steak."

He nodded. "Yes, but if you eat that heavy then sometimes the food doesn't sit well if the sex is too, um, vigorous."

I tried not to smile and failed. "And is the sex going to be, um, vigorous?"

"I hope so," he said.

"And you got the salad, because . . ."

"I'll be doing most of the work," he said.

"Now, that's just not true," I said.

He wrapped his arms around me, and his being the same height made the eye contact very serious, very intimate.

"Who does the most work depends on who is doing what." His voice was low and deep. His face leaned closer as he said, "I know exactly what I want to do to you and with you, and it means that I will be doing"—and his mouth was just above mine—"most of the work."

I thought he'd kiss me, but he didn't. He drew back and left me breathless and a little shaky. When I could talk without sounding as wobbly as I felt, I asked, "How do you do that?"

"Do what?" he asked as he sat down on his side of the table, spreading his napkin in his lap.

I gave him a look.

He laughed. "I am your Nimir-Raj, Anita. You are my Nimir-Ra, my leopard queen. The moment we met, my beast and that part of you that calls and is called to the wereleopards were drawn to each other. You know that."

I blushed, because the memory of just how much we'd been drawn together from the moment we'd met always made me a little embarrassed. All right, more than a little.

Micah was the first man I'd ever had sex with within hours of meeting him. The only thing that had kept it from being a one-night stand was the fact that he stuck around, but I hadn't known he would when it first happened. Micah had been the first person I fed the *ardeur* off of, the first warm body that I slaked that awful thirst on. Was that the bond? Was that the foundation of it?

"You're frowning," he said.

"Thinking too hard," I said.

"And not about anything pleasant, from the look on your face."

I shrugged, which made the jacket rub on the gun. I took the jacket off and draped it across the back of the chair. Now the shoulder holster was bare and aggressive against the crimson shirt. My arms were exposed, which showed off most of my scars.

"You're angry," he said. "Why?"

I actually hung my head, because he was right. "Don't ask, okay? Just let my grumpy mood go, and I'll try to let it go, too."

He looked at me for a moment, then gave a small nod. But his face was back to being careful. His neutral, pleasant *I'm managing her moods* face. I hated that face because it meant I was being difficult, but I didn't know how to stop being difficult. I was tripping over issues I'd thought I'd worked out months ago. What the hell was the matter with me?

We ate in silence, but it wasn't companionable silence. It was strained, at least in my own head.

"Okay," Micah said, and his voice made me jump.

"What?" I asked, and my voice sounded strident, somewhere between breathy and a yell.

"I have no idea why you are this"—he made a waffling motion with his hand—"but we'll play it your way. How did you get the scars on your left arm?"

I looked down at my arm as if it had suddenly

appeared there. I stared at the mound of scar tissue at the inside of the elbow, the cross-shaped burn scar just below it, the knife cut, and the newer bite marks between the two. Those bites were still sort of pink, not white and shiny like the rest. Okay, the burn wasn't white, darker actually, but . . . "Which one?" I asked, looking up at him.

He smiled then. "The cross-shaped burn scar."

I shrugged. "I got captured by some Renfields—humans with a few bites—who belonged to a master vampire. The Renfields chained me up as a sort of snack for when their master rose for the night, but while we were waiting they decided to have some fun. The fun was heating up a cross-shaped branding iron and marking me."

"You tell the story like it doesn't mean anything to you."

I shrugged again. "It doesn't. Not really. I mean it was scary and horrible, and hurt like hell. I try not to think about it. If I dwell too much on the things that could go wrong or have gone wrong in the past, I have trouble doing my job."

He looked at me, and he was angry. I didn't know why. "How would you feel if I told my story the same way?"

"Tell your story any way you want, or don't tell it, Micah. I'm not the one forcing us to play true confessions."

"Fine," he said. "I was eighteen, almost nineteen. It was the fall I went away to college. My cousin Richie had just gotten back from basic. We both came home so we could go hunting with our dads one last time. You know, one last boys' weekend out." His voice held anger, and I finally realized that he wasn't angry at me.

"At the last minute, Dad couldn't come with us. Some hunters had gone missing, and Dad thought one of his patrols had found them."

"Your dad was a cop?"

He nodded. "County sheriff. The body they found turned out to be a homeless guy who got lost in the woods and died of exposure. Some animals got to him, but they hadn't killed him."

His face had gone distant with remembering. I'd

had a lot of people tell me awful truths, and he told it like most of them did, no hysterics. No anything, really. No effect, as the therapists and the profilers would say. He looked empty as he told his story. Not matter-of-fact the way I told my story, but empty, as if part of him wasn't really there. The only thing that showed the strain was that thread of anger in his voice.

"We were all armed, and Uncle Steve and Dad had taught Richie and me how to use a gun. I could shoot before I could ride a bike." He set his silverware down on the table, and his fingers found the salt shaker. It was real glass, smooth and elegant for a salt shaker. He turned it around and around in his fingers, giving it all his eye contact.

"We knew it might be the last time the four of us got to hunt together, you know? College for me, the army for Richie—it was all changing. Dad was really upset that he didn't get to come, and so was I. Uncle Steve offered to wait, but Dad told him to go ahead. We wouldn't all get our deer in one day. He was going to drive up and join us the next day."

He paused again, this time for so long that I thought he'd stopped for good. I gave him the silence to decide. Stop, or go; tell or not.

His voice when it came was emptier; no anger now, but the soft beginnings of something worse. "We'd gotten a doe. We always got two buck tags and two doe tags, so between the four of us, we could shoot what we found." He frowned, then looked at me. "You don't know what a deer tag is, do you?"

"The deer tag tells you what you can shoot, buck or doe. You don't get a choice some years, because some years there are more does than bucks, so they give out more doe tags. Though usually it's buck that's more plentiful."

He looked surprised. "You've been deer hunting."

I nodded. "My dad used to take me."

He smiled. "Beth, my sister, thought it was barbaric. We were killing Bambi. My brother, Jeremiah— Jerry—didn't like killing things. Dad didn't hold it against him, but it meant that Dad and I were closer than him and Jerry, you know?"

I nodded. "I know." And just like that he'd told me more about his family than I'd ever known. I hadn't even known he'd had siblings.

He kept his eyes on my face now. He stared right at me as he said the next part, stared so hard that even under normal circumstances it would have been difficult to hold his gaze. Now, like this, it was like lifting some great weight just to meet the demand in his eyes. I did it, but it was hard work.

"We had a doe. We'd field dressed it and put it on a pole. Richie and I were carrying it. Uncle Steve was a little ahead of us. He was carrying Richie's gun and his. I had my rifle on a strap across my back. Dad always told me that if it was my gun, I needed to hold on to it. I had to control it at all times. Funny. I don't think Dad really liked guns."

His face started to break, not badly, but around the edges. All the emotions that he was trying not to have chased around the borders of his face. If you didn't know what you were looking at, you might not have understood it, but I'd had too many people tell me too many awful things not to see it.

"It was a beautiful day. The sun was warm, the sky was blue, the aspens were like gold. The wind was gusty that day. It kept blowing the leaves around in showers of gold. It was like standing inside a snow globe except instead of snow, it was golden, yellow leaves. God, it was beautiful. And that was when it came for us. It moved so fast, just a dark blur. It hit Uncle Steve and he just went down, never got back up." His eyes were a little wide, his pulse jumping enough in his throat that I could see it. But other than that his face was neutral. Control—such tight control.

"Richie and I dropped the deer, but Richie didn't have a gun. I got my rifle almost to my shoulder when it hit Richie. He went down screaming, but he drew his knife. He tried to fight back. I saw the knife sparkling in the sunlight."

He stopped again, and this time the pause was so long that I said, "You can stop, if you want to."

"Is it too horrible for you?"

I frowned and shook my head. "No, if you want to tell it, I'll listen."

"I made a big deal out of this, not you. My own fault." He said that last word with more feeling than it needed. *Fault.* I could taste the survivor's guilt on the air.

I wanted to go around the table and touch him but was afraid to. I wasn't sure he wanted to be touched while he told the story. Later, but not now.

"You know how time can freeze in the middle of a fight?"

I nodded, wasn't sure he saw it, and said, "Yes."

"I remember the face, its face, when it looked up at me from Richie's body. You've seen us in half-man form. The face is leopard, but not. Not human, but not animal either. I remember thinking, *I should know what this is*. But all I could think was *Monster. It's a monster.*"

He licked his lips and drew a breath that shook when he let it out. "I had the rifle to my shoulder. I fired. I hit it. I hit it two or three times before it got me. It ripped me with its claws, and it wasn't a sharp pain. It was like being hit with a baseball bat—hard, thick. You know you're hurt, but it doesn't feel like you'd imagine claws would feel—do you know what I mean?"

I nodded. "Yeah, actually, I know exactly what you mean."

He looked at me, then down at my arm. "You do know what I mean, exactly what I mean, don't you?"

"More than most," I said, voice soft and as matter-of-fact as I could make it. He had so much emotion that I gave him none back. It was the best I could do.

He smiled at me. Again it was that sad, wistful, self-deprecating smile. "The rifle was gone. I don't remember losing it, but my arms wouldn't work anymore. I lay there on the ground, with that thing above me, and I wasn't afraid anymore. Nothing hurt, nothing scared me. It was almost peaceful. After that it's only snatches. I remember voices, being on a stretcher. I remember being put in a helicopter. I woke up in the hospital with Agent Fox on one side and my dad on the other."

I realized then what had sparked the trip down memory lane. "Seeing Fox today brought it back." Some days I'm just slow.

He nodded. "It scared me to see him, Anita. I know that sounds stupid, but it did."

"It doesn't sound stupid, and it didn't show. I mean, even I didn't pick up on it."

"I wasn't afraid in the front of my head, Anita. I was afraid in the back of my head. And then you didn't like the room, and—"

I went to him then. I wrapped my arms around him, pressed his face against my chest. He hugged me back, tight, so tight, as if he were holding on to the last solid thing in the universe.

"I love the room. I love you. I'm sorry I was shitty."

He spoke with his face still buried against my body, so his words were muffled. "I didn't survive the attack, Anita. The wereleopard that attacked us ate as much of my uncle and Richie as it could hold, and left. Some hunters found us, and they were both doctors. I was dead, Anita. No heartbeat, no pulse. The doctors got my heart started again, got me breathing again. They patched me up as best they could, and they got me to a clearing so a chopper could get me to a hospital. No one expected me to live."

I stroked his hair, still slick and tight in the braid. "But you did," I whispered.

He nodded, rubbing his head against the silk shirt and my breasts underneath. Not sexual, but comforting.

"The wereleopard was a serial killer. He hit only hunters, and only after they'd killed an animal. The FBI put out a warning to hunters after we were attacked. Fox said they put it together as a serial case only a few hours before we were attacked. The first attack had been on a reservation where he was assigned."

"He solved it," I said.

"He caught the . . . monster. He was there when they killed it."

He kept saying *it* and *monster*. You didn't hear that often from shapeshifters—not about other shifters. "I died, was brought back, survived, and healed. Healed so fast. Incredibly fast. Then a month later I was the monster." His voice was so sad when he said it, so unutterably sad.

"You're not a monster," I said.

He drew away enough to look up at me. "But a lot

of us are, Anita. I joined Merle's pard, and he was a good leader, but Chimera came and took us over, and Chimera was crazy and cruel."

Chimera had been the leader I'd killed to save Micah and his people, and a lot of other people. Chimera had been the only panwere that I'd ever heard of, someone who could turn into a variety of animals. Before I'd seen him I'd have said it was impossible, but I'd seen him, and had to destroy him. He'd been real and powerful, and a very creative sexual sadist.

I held his face in my hands. "You are a good person, Micah. You are not a monster."

"I used you when we first met, Anita. I saw you as a way to save my leopards. To rescue us all."

"I know," I said. "We talked about it. You asked me what I would have done to save Nathaniel and all the leopards from Chimera. I agreed that I would have done anything, or at least what you did to get me involved. I couldn't fault you on it."

"From the moment you touched me, the plan changed. You changed it. You changed everything.

You never looked at me like I was a monster. You were never afraid of me, not in any way."

"You make it sound like someone else was afraid of you."

He sighed again. "I had a high school sweetheart. We weren't exactly engaged, but we had an understanding that once we got our college degrees, we'd marry."

"Sounds good," I said.

He shook his head. "We waited for sex, a year of waiting. We both wanted to be out of high school first, be eighteen. Her older sister had gotten pregnant in high school, and it had wrecked her life, so Becky was careful. I was okay with that. I planned to spend the rest of my life with her, so what was a year or more?"

He spilled me down into his lap so I was sitting across his legs, very ladylike, thank you. "What happened?" I asked, because he seemed to want me to.

"What made her finally break up completely with me was me being a monster. She couldn't love an animal."

I couldn't keep the shock off my face. "Jesus, Micah, that's—"

He nodded. "It was rough, but me being a shapeshifter was the last straw, not the first one."

I frowned a little. "What was the first straw?"

He looked down, and I realized he was embarrassed.

"What?" I asked.

"I was too big."

I opened my mouth and closed it. "You mean you were too well endowed for her?"

He nodded.

I looked at him and tried to decide what to say. Nothing good came to mind. "She didn't like having sex with you?"

"No."

"But—but you're, like, amazing in bed. You're—"

"But you weren't a virgin, and I wasn't eighteen and a virgin, too."

"Oh," I said, and thought about it. Micah was very well endowed. Not just long but wide, which I'd discovered could be a harder problem to deal with than length. There were positions you could do or modify for length. Width you just had to adjust to. I thought about having all that shoved inside for the first time, maybe without enough foreplay. "I guess I can see the problem."

"I hurt her. I didn't mean to, but I did. I got better at it. More foreplay, more—just better."

"There is a learning curve," I said.

He rested his forehead on my shoulder. "But Becky never really enjoyed me inside her. We had sex, but I always had to be so careful of her or she said it hurt."

"You know women have different sizes of vaginas, just like there are different sizes of penises. Maybe she was small inside, and you are *not* small."

He looked up at me, his cheek resting on my bare arm. "You think so?"

"I do."

He smiled. "You don't have a problem with me, any of me."

I smiled back. "No, and she was just one person. One negative doesn't make it a problem."

"It wasn't just one vote, Anita."

I raised my eyebrows. "What do you mean?"

"I've had dates in college where everything was fine until they saw me, all of me. Then they picked up their clothes and said no way."

I gave him a look. "You're serious."

He nodded.

Another man, I might have accused of bragging, but Micah wasn't bragging. I had a thought. It was almost insightful. "Becky said you hurt her because you were so big, and then you had girls in college who wouldn't even try it. That must have really messed with you."

"It was either a really big plus or a really big minus with women. But most of them, even the ones who said yes, didn't want a standard diet. I was like a novelty." His voice held unhappiness the way it had held anger earlier. "Becky made me feel like a monster for wanting to hurt her, for wanting to be inside her, for wanting sex so badly I'd hurt her. Most of the women I dated made me feel the same way, or like I should have had a dial on my hip and a battery case, like I was some sort of toy they'd bought in a sex store. Just wind me up."

I looked at him again.

"Trust me, Anita, there are just as many bastards out there who are girls as bastards who are guys. Except when a girl treats you like a sex object, it's supposed to be all right because you're a guy and you only want sex anyway, right?"

"The old double standard," I said.

He nodded and patted me. "Until you."

I thought about it for a second. "Wait a minute. How did you know I wouldn't have a problem with your, um, size?"

"You know how wereanimals are always walking around naked, unless you make us put on clothes?"

I smiled. "Not all of you guys are comfortable nudists, but most, yeah."

"First, I'd seen Richard nude, and I knew he had been your lover. He isn't small either." I fought not to blush again. "Second, you'd seen me nude and you hadn't reacted badly."

"So you saw an ex-lover and he was well endowed. And I hadn't told you to be careful where you point that. It might go off."

He smiled. "Something like that."

"How did you know that I hadn't broken up with Richard because he was too much man for me to handle?"

"I asked."

I must have looked as surprised as I felt.

He laughed. "I didn't ask Richard. I asked around and found out he thought you were too bloodthirsty, and he didn't like the police work. None of that bothered me."

"So you took a chance," I said.

He nodded. "And from the moment we made love, I knew I would do anything, anything, to be in your life."

"You said that. It was one of the first things you ever said to me after we'd had sex. That you were my Nimir-Raj, and I was your Nimir-Ra, and you would do anything, be anything I needed, to be in my life."

"I meant it."

"I know you did." I traced my finger down the side of his face. "Admittedly, it took me a while to realize that you really did mean it. That you would do anything, be anything I needed. What if I'd asked awful things of you, Micah? What would you have done?"

"You wouldn't ask awful things of anyone."

"But you barely knew me then."

"I just had a feeling."

I searched his expression, trying to see where that certainty had come from. His face was back to being peaceful but not empty. This was his peaceful *I'm happy* face.

"I would never have been able to trust a stranger like that."

"We were never strangers, Anita. From the moment we touched, we weren't strangers. Our bodies knew each other."

I gave him the hard look, but he just laughed. "Tell me I'm wrong. Tell me that isn't how you felt, too."

I opened my mouth, closed it, and finally said, "So what? Not love at first sight, but love at first fuck?"

His face went all serious on me. "Don't make fun of it, Anita."

I had to look down then, sitting chastely on his thighs, and I had to look away. "I did feel it, that draw to your body, from the first time we touched.

It's just . . . I was raised believing that sex was bad, dirty. The fact that you got through all my defenses so quickly still sort of embarrasses me."

He put his arms around me and scooted me higher up his lap, so I could feel that he was happy to have me there. Just feeling how hard he was, pressed against my thigh, made me catch my breath.

"Never be embarrassed about how your body re-acts, Anita. It's a gift." He slid his arm under my legs and stood up with me in his arms.

"I can walk," I said.

"I want to carry you."

I opened my mouth to tell him to put me down but didn't. "Where are you carrying me to?"

"To the bed," he said.

I tried not to smile, but it was a losing battle.

"Why?" Though I was pretty sure I knew why.

"So we can have sex, lots and lots of sex, and when we've had as much sex as we can stand, you can drop your shields and feed the *ardeur* now, early, so it doesn't try to rise while we're surrounded by FBI agents." He started carrying me toward the bed again.

He carried me easily, smoothly, even though there probably wasn't twenty pounds' difference in our weight.

I said the only thing I could think of. "You do know how to sweet-talk a girl."

He grinned at me. "Well, I could have said that I plan on fucking you until you're unconscious, but then you'd just think I was bragging."

"I've never passed out during sex," I said.

"There's got to be a first time," he said. And we were at the foot of the bed now.

"Talk is cheap," I said.

He threw me on the bed. Threw me suddenly and far enough that I did that squeaky girlish scream when I bounced on the bed. My pulse was in my throat suddenly. He had his tie undone and was working on the buttons of his shirt. "Bet I'll be naked first."

"No fair," I said. "I've got the shoulder holster to get off."

He was pushing the silk suspenders off his shoulders and pulling his shirt out of his pants. "Then you better hurry."

I hurried.

CHAPTER

7

Micah lay back on the bed while I was still struggling out of my clothes. Seeing him naked against the pillows and the gold and white of the bedspread made me stop and stare. And, no, I didn't only stare at his groin. How could I stare at just one thing when all of him was lying there?

He didn't look that muscular clothed. You had to see him at least mostly naked to appreciate the fine play of muscle in his arms, chest, stomach, legs. Clothed, he looked delicate, especially for a man. Nude, he looked strong and somehow more . . . more something that clothes stole from him. His tan was dark against the cream of the bedspread, making his body stand out like it had been drawn there. His shoulders were wide, his waist and hips narrow. He was built like a swimmer, but it was his natural shape, not from any particular sport that he did.

I missed the spill of his hair around his face, but he'd left it in its braid, and I didn't tell him to take it down. Sometimes it was good not to have all that hair flying loose. It could get in the way.

I let my gaze settle last on the swell of him, so hard, so long. Long enough that he could touch his own belly button without using his hands. Thick enough that I couldn't get finger and thumb completely around him when he was at his thickest. I came back up to his face and met those eyes, the delicate curve of his face.

"You are so beautiful," I said.

He smiled. "Shouldn't that be my line?"

I pulled at the garter belt. "You want me to leave this and the hose on, or take them off?"

"Can you get the underwear off without the garter coming off?" he asked.

I put my thumbs under the edge of the lace panties and slipped them off. Jean-Claude had broken me of wearing the panties on the inside. He said that was only for looks. For real, you put the panties on last, so they can come off first. I didn't say that out loud, because I wasn't sure Micah really wanted to be reminded right now that I was having sex with other men. He shared well and didn't seem to mind, but talking about another lover in the midst of sex just seemed bad form.

I stood there for a moment in nothing but the garter belt, the hose, and the heels. I stood there until his eyes filled with that darkness that men's eyes fill with in the moment they realize you won't say no. There is something of possession in that look, something that says *mine*. I can't explain it, but I've seen enough to know that all men do it, at least part of the time. Do women have a look that's similar? Maybe. Did I? Without a mirror I might never know.

He crawled across the bed to me and said, "Come here." His hand wrapped around my wrist, pulling me against the bed, but I had to climb up on it, had to let him help pull me onto it.

He led me until we crawled to the head of the bed. He pulled me onto all those pillows. So many pillows, so high, that I was propped up against them. I was almost sitting up. Almost.

I expected Micah to lie down with me, but he didn't.

He knelt and said, "Bend your knees."

I wasn't exactly sure what he had in mind, but I bent my knees firmly together, curling my legs, heels and all, against the front of my body. It felt very posed, but the smile on his face made it worth it. The smile said that I'd done exactly what he wanted me to do. He laid his hands on the top of the hose and ran them down that silky length until his hands curled around my ankles. He spread my legs with his hands on my ankles, spread me wide. He put my feet in the high heels to either side, knees bent. Apparently my legs weren't quite wide enough, because he spread them just a little wider.

He leaned back from me on his knees and just looked down at me. "Wow," he said, and his voice came out in a hoarse growl. An innocent word, said in a tone that made it anything but innocent.

"God, what a view." And his voice was still that low, growling bass, as if it should have hurt to talk. He trailed his hands down my thighs until he ran out of hose and traced fingertips along my bare thighs. He slid his hands under my buttocks, cupping my ass. He lay down with his hands still cupped under my body. He propped himself up on his elbows and stared up the length of my body at me.

My voice was breathy. "That's why you kept the braid in."

"Yes," he whispered, and began to lower his face down toward me, the way you'd move in slowly for a kiss. He hesitated. "The angle's not quite right." He lifted me up, as if he could hold me forever in his hands like an offering to himself. My feet came off the bed with his lifting. I was left with the choice of either holding my own legs up with my hands or putting my feet around Micah. If I hadn't been wearing high heels I wouldn't have worried about it, but the heels were not meant to stab into someone's back. Nathaniel might have enjoyed it, but Micah wouldn't.

He licked between my legs and the sensation stole my thoughts, my words, and my good intentions. I put my legs around his body. The shoes ended up resting on his lower back, the toes on the swell of his buttocks, the tip of the heels pressed into his back.

I waited for him to protest, but he didn't. He slid his face between my thighs, plunged his mouth into me, against me, over me. He kissed between my legs as if it were my mouth. Exploring with lips, tongue, and, lightly, teeth. He kissed me as if I could kiss him back, and the sensation of it made me move my hips against him, so that it became like a kiss. A kiss of his mouth between my legs, my hips rolling up to his mouth, my thighs pressing against his face, my heels digging into his back.

I felt a spasm pass up his body, shivering up his

back, his shoulders, to his hands, making his fingers tighten around my ass.

He raised up enough to talk, his mouth shining. His voice was breathy, strained. "I can't decide if the heels feel amazing, or just hurt. Can we lose them?"

I scraped one shoe off on the bedspread and used that foot to push the other shoe off. I put my feet back on his back, feeling the warmth and swell of him through the hose. "All you had to do was ask." My voice was breathless and lower than normal. It's called a bedroom voice for a reason.

He smiled at me and lowered his face slowly downward. He kept his gaze on my face as he slid between my thighs. Those chartreuse eyes rolled up to me as he licked between my legs, so that it gave the illusion that his face ended with the green-gold of his eyes.

"God, Micah, I love your eyes like that."

He growled, and the sound of it vibrated across my skin. It made me cry out, head back, eyes closed. The growl turned to a purr as he drew the most intimate part of me deeper into his mouth. That purring growl sang across my skin, vibrating, building. He drew as much of me into his mouth as he could and sucked as hard and fast as he could.

That heavy, delicious warmth began to build between my legs. Micah drew that warmth, that weight of pleasure with his mouth, drawing it out and out, more and more, building it with every movement of his lips, every caress of his tongue, until with one last flick of his tongue he brought me. That weight burst over me in a rush of warm pleasure that pulsed through me, over me, again and again as if as long as Micah sucked, the pleasure would never stop. I was left gasping, eyes fluttered shut, boneless, helpless. I was wrecked, ruined, drowned in the pleasure of it. I felt the bed move, felt Micah over me. I tried to open my eyes, but the best I could do was flutter them enough to see light and shadows.

"Anita," he said, voice soft, "are you all right?"

I tried to say yes, but no sound came out. I could think it, but that was as far as I got.

"Anita, say something. Blink if you can hear me."

I managed to blink, but even when my eyes fluttered open, I still couldn't focus. The world was blurred colors. I put up a thumb to let him know I was okay, because talking was still too hard.

He leaned close enough that I could see his face clearly. "Now I'm going to fuck you," he said.

I managed to whisper, "Yes, please, yes."

CHAPTER

8

He put his hands under my thighs and pulled me off the mound of pillows. Pulled me so that my lower body was flat to the bed, but my upper body was still a little propped up. He put a finger inside of me, just a finger, but the sensation of it writhed me across the bed, made me cry out.

"So wet, but so tight. You're always so tight after I do you by mouth."

He was kneeling between my legs, his body so hard, so ripe, so ready. I said the only thing I was thinking.

"Fuck me, Micah, fuck me."

"You're tight, Anita, really tight."

I raised up on my elbows. "But wet. I'm so wet. You've made me so wet."

He licked his lips and swallowed. I could see his pulse jumping in his throat. "I don't want to hurt you."

"If it hurts, I'll say so."

He looked down at me, and his face didn't look lustful now; it looked nervous, uncertain. I knew he wanted to try to shove himself inside me, but he was afraid to. How many women had hurt him? How many had told him he was a freak, a monster, simply because he was so very male? I sat up enough to wrap my hand around the hard length of him. Just holding it in my hand threw my head back, made me cry out. I stared at him, knowing my eyes were wild, squeezing my hand around him until his head went back, his eyes rolled into his head.

I slid my hand up over him, caressing the soft, luscious head. I leaned back on my elbows, looking at him. "Fuck me, Micah. Fuck me before I stop having little spasms inside me. You made me so wet, so tight, my body is still having little mini orgasms. I want you inside me while my body is still spasming."

He bent over and kissed me, his mouth still wet from me, still tasting like meat and that fresh taste, almost like rain. People can make fish jokes, but not every woman tastes the same.

He drew back from the kiss, kept himself propped up on his arms. But his body was already pushing against me.

Feeling the weight of him against me made me fall back against the bed. He kept his body above mine so I could see every inch of him as he began to try to push his way inside me.

I was wet enough, but he was so wide, so very wide, that he had to ease his way in, and even easing had a level of force to it. He had to force his way in. If I'd released the *ardeur*, I would have been more open, more ready for him. The *ardeur* alone without much foreplay could make my body ready, eager, and more open. But we both wanted me tight, both wanted to feel him fight his way inside me.

The tip vanished inside me, with so much left still. Watching him push inch by inch inside me made me cry out, made my body rise up, so that my hands went around my own thighs. So that I held my legs up and made my body a little ball. So I could see, and feel, all of it.

Halfway through his eyes closed, and he stopped moving, head down. His voice came strained. "So wet. God, so tight. You keep gripping me with your body. It's like the farther in I push, the more you spasm. Just me pushing inside you, causing small orgasms."

"Yes," I said, and my voice was breathy, it was eager. "Yes, the sensation of you inside me, when I'm this tight, this wet. It's amazing. Oh, God, Micah, don't stop, don't stop."

He raised his face up then and met my eyes. He searched my face as if he thought I was lying to him.

"You're serious?"

"Yes, God, yes."

"You're wet enough, but we've never tried this when you were this tight, Anita." Eagerness fought in his eyes with worry. "I can push in faster, but I don't want to hurt you."

I stared into his face and said what I was thinking. "I don't know whose ghost you're fighting right now, but it's not me. Whoever you thought you hurt, it wasn't me. Fuck me, fuck me, fuck me the way we both want you to."

I watched him decide with our faces inches apart, our bodies already wedded to each other. I watched him decide. His hips moved forward, shoved himself inside me. I'd told him to stop being careful. He took me at my word.

He shoved himself inside me, fought to push his hardness inside me, as far and as fast as he could. I was too tight and he was too wide for speed, but whereas before when he felt resistance he'd hesitated, now he shoved harder. My body resisted, and his body crashed through. He shoved all that hard, wide meat inside me. He forced his way in, while my body was still trying to figure out if it was a good thing or a bad thing.

On one hand it felt amazing, so hard, so long, so wide, and all inside me. God, it felt good. It flung me back against the bed, tore screams of pleasure from my mouth. It made me writhe around him, wriggling and struggling, caught between orgasm and my body telling me that maybe we shouldn't be doing this. About the time I thought, *Too much, too wide, slow down,* and actually drew breath to say it, the orgasm stopped being spasms and was suddenly full-blown. It caught me off guard as a lot of intercourse orgasms did. It turned almost-pain to unbelievable pleasure. It made me throw my body around him, over him, fling my upper body against the pillows, over and over again like a puppet whose strings had been cut. I writhed and screamed, and fought, and danced under him. And he shoved himself as far inside me as he could, hitting the end of me when there was still some of him yet to go.

He drew himself out of me, and it rubbed, because orgasm was tightening me around him, trying to hold on to all of him as he pulled back out. He began to shove himself inside again as far and hard as the tightness would let him. He fought his way in and out, while I writhed and screamed. I had to hold on to something. My hands found his shoulders, his arms, and drew blood down them. Too much pleasure, too many sensations, as if all that pleasure spilled out of me in the blood that ran down his body.

His voice came gasping. "Feed the *ardeur* soon, Anita, please. God, soon. I'm not going to last much longer." I'd forgotten what we were doing. I'd forgotten about the *ardeur*. I'd forgotten everything but the sex. It took only a thought, and the *ardeur* was suddenly there. But I was too far gone in orgasm, pleasure, our bodies. Always before, the *ardeur* had felt like more, like its own presence, but now it was only another part of the sex. It was like an extra layer of heat added to a bonfire that was already burning down the room.

It tore sounds from my throat, raked my nails down Micah's back, and only then did I realize he was on top of me, not above me, but pressed on top of me in a more standard missionary position. I hadn't remembered when he changed position.

The *ardeur* had opened me to him, and he was finally able to shove himself in and out of me, not fighting my body now but sliding in and out. He came to the end of me before his thrust was finished, but there was no more of me, nowhere else for him to go. He raised up on his arms for a moment so I could gaze down my body at the meat of him going inside me, over and over and over, and the orgasm was almost, almost, almost. I could feel his body changing rhythm, feel that he was close. The *ardeur* couldn't feed off of Micah until he orgasmed. He was too dominant, too controlled; only orgasm let his shields down enough to be food for me.

He cried out above me, his hips doing one last thrust that brought me screaming off the bed, bowing my back, closing my eyes. I screamed for him a long time after he had finished, and he lay on top of me, trying to relearn how to breathe. I screamed and writhed underneath him, still caught in the aftershocks of what we'd done.

When he could move, he pulled out of me, and that made me writhe again, but almost as soon as he was out the ache began. That the endorphins had begun to fade that fast meant I'd be sore later. But it was the kind of sore I didn't mind. The kind of sore that would be like a keepsake, that I could take out and look at and remember what we'd done. I'd remember the pleasure of it with every ache between my legs.

Micah lay oddly, half on his stomach, half on his side. The arm that was toward me was bleeding. He'd have his own aches and pains to remember this by. He moved, propping himself up on his elbows, and I saw his back.

I gasped and said, "Jesus, Micah, I'm sorry."

He winced. "The nails don't usually hurt this soon after great sex."

I nodded. "When the endorphins go quick, you know you're hurt." His back looked like he'd been attacked by something with more claws than I had.

"Are you hurting?" he asked.

"A little ache."

He gave me serious eyes. "When I drew out, there was blood. Not much, but some."

"We've had color before," I said.

"Yeah, but that's usually near your period. This isn't." His face was serious again. That shadow of old memories, old girlfriends in his eyes.

"How does your back feel?" I asked.

He grinned for me. "It hurts."

"Do you regret it?"

He shook his head. "God, no, it was a-fucking-mazing."

"Ask me how I feel," I said.

"Did I hurt you?"

"I ache already, which means a little." I touched his face before he could look away. "Now ask me if I regret it."

He gave me that sad, mixed smile of his. "Do you regret it?"

"God, no," I said. "You were a-fucking-mazing."

He smiled then, and it was a real smile. I watched the ghosts fade from his eyes until there was nothing but warm pleasure left.

"I love you," he said. "I love you so much."

"And I love you."

He looked down at the bedspread, which was a

little worse for wear. "I better get up off this before we get more blood on it." He got to his feet, steadying himself on the edge of the bed as if his legs weren't quite working yet. I couldn't have walked if a fire alarm had gone off, so I sympathized.

There were spots of blood here and there, almost outlining the upper part of his body. There was also a spot of crimson where his lower body had been pressed to the bedspread. White had been a bad choice for it. I pushed myself up enough to look down at my own body. There was blood between my legs and a little on the bedspread below my body. "Think the maid will call the cops?" I asked.

He started a shaky walk toward the door. I think he was headed for the bathroom. "Not if we tip her enough." He caught the door as if he'd have fallen without it.

"Careful," I said.

He leaned against the door for a moment, then looked at me. "You make everything all right for me, Anita. You make me feel like a human being instead of a monster."

"And you love all of me, Micah, every last hard-boiled, ruthless bit of me. You make it okay that sometimes I am the monster. You know what I do, and you still love me."

"You're not a monster, Anita"—he grinned at me—"but you are ruthless. But then I like that in a girl." He went toward the bathroom still a little shaky but moving better. I settled back on the bed and waited for my knees and thighs to work enough to walk. I might as well get comfortable; it was going to be a while before I could move.

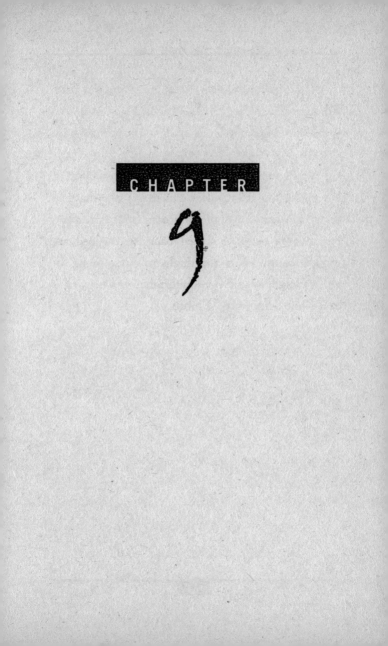

CHAPTER

9

Philly was a pretty city, what little I'd seen of it. The visit so far had consisted of the airport and the hotel room and some amazing sex. We could have been anywhere. The cemetery reminded me that the city was in one of the thirteen original colonies. It was old, that cemetery. It breathed its age and the age of its dead. Breathed it along my skin the moment we stepped out of Fox's car. Once, a cemetery this old would have been peaceful for me. Too old to have ghosts, maybe a few shivery spots if you walked directly over a grave, but mostly the dead here would be inert, earth to earth, dust to dust, and all that. But now the dead called to me, even through my shielding.

Theoretically, no one could raise the long dead without a human sacrifice. I probably held the record for oldest without one, but even two-hundred-plus years dead should have been beyond me. So why, lately, did the long dead whisper power across my skin?

I shivered, but it wasn't from the early November cold. In fact, I was too warm in the leather jacket. Micah was suddenly at my side. He helped me slip the jacket off, whispering, "Are you all right?"

I nodded. I was all right, better than all right. Standing there in the power-kissed darkness was intoxicating. It was as if my skin were drinking magic from the very air. Which, with necromancy, wasn't possible.

Micah asked Fox if we could put the jacket back in the car. I didn't wait to hear what Fox said; I was already walking out into the dark. I absently trailed my fingers along the weathered tops of the tombstones as I walked between them.

Old cemeteries are crowded things. The ground was smooth and rough, but there was no longer much to differentiate ground from grave, so that I walked one step on the ground, then on the second step walked over a grave. You know the old saying *Someone walked over my grave?* This was like the reverse of that. I didn't feel bad, or shaky, or scared. With every grave I walked over, I felt better, steadier, more confident. I took a little energy from every body I passed over, no matter how old. I could have drunk in the power of the dead underneath me and done . . . Done what?

The thought stopped me literally in my tracks. What I hadn't realized was that Franklin was following me, close. I hadn't even known he was there.

He ran into me, or nearly. He had to grab my arms to keep from smacking into the back of me. It startled both of us. He apologized before I'd finished turning around.

"I'm sorry, I didn't know you were . . . stopping." He sounded breathless and way more upset than he should have been.

I was left staring up at him, wondering why he was nervous. Then I saw what he was doing with his hands. He was running them up and down the sleeves of his trench coat, as if he'd touched something and was trying to wipe it off. He wasn't being insulting. I doubt he even realized he was doing it. I might have done the same thing if I'd touched someone else's magic unexpectedly. It was like walking through metaphysical cobwebs; you had to brush it off. He had felt at least some of the power I was getting off the graves.

I might have asked Franklin why he'd been hiding that he was psychic, but Fox and Micah came up to us, and somehow I didn't think Franklin would want me being that insightful in front of them. Had he told the FBI that he was talented? I was betting not. It had been a plus in only the last two, three years tops. Before that they looked at it as a psychological disorder. You didn't get to be a federal agent with a psychological disorder.

It did explain why he had a serious dislike of me. If he was hiding what he was, he wouldn't want to be around someone who complemented his talents, whatever they might be. No, if you were hiding, you didn't want to be around people who were out of the broom closet, as it were.

"Is there a problem?" Fox asked.

Franklin said, "No, no problem," a little too fast.

I just shook my head, still looking up at the taller man.

I don't think Fox believed us, but he let it go. We weren't talking, so he was out of options. He gave us both a look, then said, "Then if there's no problem, everyone is waiting for us."

I nodded again, then thought to ask, "Is Rose's grave the newest one in this cemetery?"

Fox thought about it, then nodded. "Yes, why?"

I smiled at him and knew that it was a dreamy smile, as if I were listening to music he couldn't hear. "Just wanted to know what I was looking for, that's all."

"I can take you to the grave, Marshal. You don't need to look for it."

I wanted to look for it. I wanted to walk the cemetery a tombstone at a time and find it myself.

Micah answered for me. "That would be good, Fox. Lead the way."

I looked at him and fought to make it friendly. He gave me a look in return that was a warning. In the dark, with all the trees around, I doubted anyone else could have seen his expression as clearly as I did. But we both had better-than-normal night vision, though I doubted mine could compare to his kitty-cat eyes. Those eyes were bare for all to see now. Too dark for his black-lensed sunglasses, but you'd be surprised how many people wouldn't notice the strangeness of his eyes. Even in full light, a lot of people wouldn't see his eyes for what they were. People see what they want to see, unless forced to see the truth.

I looked full into his eyes and read the warning there, the worry. Was I really all right? the look asked.

The truth was yes and no. I felt great, but it was the kind of great that could go south fast and hard. One minute fine, the next moment the power could do something unfortunate.

I took a deep breath and tried to center and ground, the way I'd been taught, but that was a skill I'd learned from a psychic and witch. Her talents ran to prophecy and empathy so finely tuned it was almost telepathy. She didn't raise the dead. She didn't truly understand my talent.

Drawing myself into the center of my body was great—I felt steadier, more myself and less power-fuzzed—but the moment I tried to ground all that power into the earth, to bleed some of it off, it turned. Turned so that it didn't go deep but out and away. My power chased through the ground so that I sensed the graves, all the graves, like I was the center of a great wheel. The graves were the points along the spokes, and I knew them all. I didn't drop my shields that I hid behind to keep the dead from bothering me. The shields were just not there.

I'd known that my power was growing, but I hadn't truly understood what that might mean until right this second. I knew the dead in every grave here. I knew which still had a remnant of energy. What graves would have shivery spots if you walked over them, the last gasp of what had once been a ghost. Most of the graves were quiet, only bones and rags and dust. I'd been able to stand in a cemetery and do this for years. But what had changed was: one, I hadn't done it on purpose, and two, every grave I touched was a little more energetic for my power having breathed over it. That was new.

"Stop it, Blake." Franklin's voice was tight with anxiety.

I looked at him. "Stop what?" I asked, but my voice was lazy with power.

"Don't toy with him, Anita," Micah said.

"I'm missing something," Fox said.

I nodded. "Yeah, you are." I could have let Franklin's cat out of the bag, but I didn't. I knew what it felt like to be different and to want nothing, absolutely nothing, as much as simply to be normal. I'd given up on that a long time ago. It wasn't possible for me and never had been. Maybe it wouldn't be possible for Franklin either, but that wasn't my call. I did the only thing I could for him. I lied.

"When Franklin and I bumped into each other, he caught an edge of my power. It happens sometimes when my shields are down." That was a lie. It happened only if your abilities were similar to mine in some way, or you were so strongly psychic in some other way that you would sense any strong psychic gift used near you. Either Franklin had abilities with the dead like mediumship, being able to talk with the recently departed. Or he was powerful in some other way. Naw. If he'd been that gifted, he wouldn't have been able to hide it. I was betting that somewhere in his background was a family member who could talk to spirits. Someone he probably hated or was embarrassed about. You dislike most in others what you hate in yourself.

Fox said, "Is that right, Franklin? You bumped into the marshal."

Franklin nodded. "Yes." One word, no emotion to it, but the relief in his eyes was too raw. He turned away from Fox, from me, to hide those relieved eyes. He knew I knew, and he knew I'd lied for him. He owed me. I hoped he understood that.

Fox looked from one of us to the other, as if he suspected we were lying, or at least hiding something. He looked at Micah and got a shrug. Fox shook his head and said, "Fine." He looked at us a heartbeat longer, then shook his head, as if he'd decided to let it go. "We're going to be the last to arrive at graveside, Marshal Blake. I don't want to leave the federal judge and the lawyers waiting too long in the middle of a cemetery, so I'll lead the way. I think it will be faster that way."

I couldn't argue the faster part. "Then lead the way, Special Agent Fox."

He gave me one more hard look. It was a good look, as those kinds of looks go. But if he thought I was going to break down and fess up because of a hard look, he was wrong. I gave him a pleasant, even eager face, but nothing helpful.

He sighed and settled his shoulders, as if his shoulder holster chafed. He started off through the cemetery. Franklin fell into line behind him without a backward glance.

Micah and I followed them. Micah had us drop back enough to whisper, "You're having trouble controlling your power tonight, aren't you?"

I nodded. "Yeah, I am."

"Why?" he asked.

I shrugged. "I'm not sure."

"Then should you be raising the dead?"

"I think it will be one of the easier raisings I've ever done. There's so much power."

He grabbed my arm. "Do you even know that you're touching every tombstone as you walk by it?"

I stood there with his hand on my arm and stared at him. "I'm what?"

"You're caressing the tops of the tombstones like you'd stroke a hand through flowers in a field."

I looked at the worry in his face and knew that he wasn't lying, but . . . "Was I?"

"Yes," he said, and his grip on my arm was suddenly almost painful.

"You're hurting me," I said.

"Does it help?"

I frowned at him, then realized what he meant. The small pain had pushed back the power. I could think about something other than the dead. My first clear thought was fear. "I don't know what's wrong tonight. I really don't. I knew I was gaining abilities from the vampires, but I didn't think it would bleed over to the zombie stuff. I mean, that's my magic, not Jean-Claude's, not Richard's. Mine. Whatever happens metaphysically, it doesn't usually mess with my basic talent."

"Should you cancel tonight?" he asked.

I licked my lips, tasting the fresh lipstick I'd put on after we'd made love. I shook my head, moving into the circle of his arms. I hugged him. "If this is a new power level, then one night won't make a difference." I held him, breathing in the warm solidity of him.

"There's always a learning curve to new abilities, Anita," he whispered into my hair. "Even if that ability is only a stronger version of something else. Do we really want the learning curve to be on the FBI's dime?"

He had a point, a good one, but . . . "I'll be able to raise this zombie, Micah."

"But what else will you raise?" he asked.

I drew back enough to see his face. "How did you understand that?"

"Isn't that what you're afraid of? Not that you can't raise the dead, but that you'll raise more than you were paid for?"

I nodded. "Yeah." I shivered and drew away so I could rub my arms. "That's exactly it."

"The protective circle is usually to keep things out," he said. "Right?"

I nodded again.

"Tonight, I think maybe it will be to keep you in."

"So I don't spread over more of the graves," I said.

"Yes," he said.

"They should have chickens waiting for me to slaughter. I know Larry would have told them to bring the livestock."

Fox yelled, "Marshal, Callahan, are you coming?"

"We'll be there in a minute," Micah called. He leaned into me, hands on my arms. "Do you really think chicken blood will keep this contained?"

"Not their blood, but their lives, yes," I said.

"I'm not sure adding fresh death to your magic tonight is a good idea."

"What choice do I have, Micah? I can make a small cut in my arm or hand and use the blood, but I'm not sure what my blood touching the graveyard will do tonight. So much power tonight, it's intoxicating."

"Then use my blood," he said.

I looked at him. "You've never shared blood for a zombie raising."

"No, but I let Jean-Claude take blood from me. How much different can it be?"

There were many answers to that, but I settled for "A lot different. I can't cloud your mind to make it not hurt."

"It's a little cut, Anita. I'm okay with it."

I sighed and hugged him again. A lot of men will date you, and some will sleep with you, and a few are content to play second fiddle to your job, but how many will literally open a vein for you? Not many.

I gave him a quick kiss. "Let's go raise Mr. Rose from the dead."

He picked up the bag with all the zombie-raising paraphernalia in it. He'd carry it. After all, he was the assistant. He needed to look useful. We finished the walk to the grave hand in hand. Maybe it wasn't professional, but I didn't care anymore. Besides, once I cut his arm open with the machete, no one would complain that he wasn't assisting me enough. No, they'd think he was more than earning his paycheck. The fact that he didn't get paid to be my assistant would be our little secret.

CHAPTER

10

One of the things in the gym bag that Micah was holding was a machete longer than my forearm. Even with a badge I might have had trouble getting it on the plane, except for the magical artifact law. Magical practitioners who earned their living from their magical talent could not be denied access to their magical tools. They were to be treated the same way as crosses, or Stars Of David. The machete had had to go through checked baggage until the Supreme Court put through the exclusion act. Made it all so much more convenient for me.

We were introduced to everyone. I gave a special nod to the court reporter, the only other woman there. I spent a lot of time being the only woman everywhere I went. I'd begun to like having other women around. It made me feel less like a freak. The only girl in the all-boys club had begun to get a little lonely of late.

The lawyers on one side were unhappy with me from the moment they saw me. How relieved they must have been when Rose died quietly of natural causes before he could testify. Now here I was, about to bring him back from the dead so he could testify after all. What's the world coming to when even the dead can testify in federal court?

Arthur Salvia was the head lawyer on the side that wasn't happy to see me. His name sounded vaguely familiar, as if he'd been in the news for something, but I couldn't place it. "Your honor, I must protest again. Mr. Rose died before he could testify in court. The testimony of a dead man is not admissible."

"I get to say what is admissible, Mr. Salvia. You'll get your chance to cross-examine the witness." He frowned and turned to me. "That is correct, Ms. Blake? The zombie will be able to be cross-examined?"

I nodded, realized he might not have the night vision to see it, and said, "Yes, your honor. The zombie will be able to answer questions and respond to cross-examination."

He nodded too, then said, "There, Mr. Salvia. You will get your chance to cross-examine Mr. Rose."

"Mr. Rose is dead, your honor. I renew my objections to this entire proceeding—"

The judge held up his hand. "Heard and noted, Mr. Salvia, but save the rest of your objections for the appeal."

Salvia settled back. He was not happy.

Micah leaned in very close to my ear and whispered, "He smells like fear."

The lawyer for the accused was allowed to be nervous, but fear? That seemed a bit strong. Was he afraid of the graveyard and the whole zombie thing, or was it something else?

There was a wire mesh cage over to one side with a chicken in it. The bird clucked softly to itself, making the sleepy noises chickens make when they're settling down for the night. The chicken wasn't afraid. It didn't know it had been brought to play blood sacrifice. Larry would have needed it. I didn't. I'd discovered that I could use a little bit of my own blood to represent the sacrifice needed to raise the dead by accident. Or necessity, after Marianne, the woman who was helping me learn to control my metaphysical abilities, had gotten grief from her coven.

She hadn't been Wiccan when I first started going to her. She'd just been psychic. Then she got religion, and suddenly she was asking if I could raise the dead without killing an animal. Something about her coven speculating that she, as my teacher, would take on some of my bad karma from doing death magic. So I tried. I could do it. The zombie wasn't always as well put together, or as smart, but it still talked and could answer questions. Good enough for government work, as they say. But constantly having cuts all over my left hand and arm got old. I refused to cut my gun hand. It hurt, and I was beginning to run out of fresh places to cut. I decided that since I ate meat anyway, it wasn't so different from slaughtering a few animals to do my job. But the whole experience had taught me that I could, if I had to, raise the newly dead without killing an animal. Very recently, I'd discovered that I didn't need *any* blood to raise a zombie sometimes.

I guess I should have known I could, because I'd accidentally raised the dead when I was younger. A beloved dog that crawled out of the grave to follow me home; a college prof that committed suicide and came to my dorm room one night.

That should have told me that the blood wasn't absolutely necessary, but I'd been taught zombie-raising by a man who needed the blood, needed the sacrifice, needed the herbal salve, and all of it. I'd done it the way I'd been taught, until recently.

I was saving the lives of a lot of livestock, but it wasn't doing my nerves any good.

The judge asked in a voice that managed to be both friendly and condescending, "Could you explain what you're about to do so we'll understand what's happening and for Elaine—Ms. Beck—to get it into the court record?" He motioned at the dark-haired woman at her little folding stool and table.

His request stopped me. In all the years I'd been raising the dead, no one had ever asked me to explain. Most people treated me like a dirty little secret. Something you may need to do, but you don't want to know the details. Like sausage making. People love eating sausage, but they don't want to know too many details about how it's made.

I closed my mouth, then managed to say, "Fine." Of course, since I'd never explained before, I wasn't sure how to explain at all. How do you explain magic to people who don't do magic? How do you explain psychic gifts to people who have none? Hell if I knew, but I tried.

"First we'll do a circle of protection," I said.

Salvia asked, "I have a question for Marshal Blake."

"She's not a witness, Mr. Salvia," the judge said.

"Without her abilities, this testimony would be impossible to retrieve. Is that not true, your honor?"

The judge seemed to think about that for a second or two. "Yes, but all I've asked of the marshal is that she explain the mechanics of what she is about to do. That isn't witness testimony."

"No, but she is an expert witness, the same as any other forensic expert."

"I'm not certain that an animator is a forensic expert, Mr. Salvia."

"But she is an expert on raising the dead, correct?"

Again the judge thought about it. He saw the trap that his little request for an explanation for the court record had gotten us into. If I had information for the court record, then my information was suddenly open to questioning by the attorneys. Shit.

"I will concede that Marshal Blake is an expert on raising the dead."

Laban, the head attorney for the other side, said, "I think we'll all agree to that. What is the defense's point?"

"If she's an expert witness, then I should be able to question her."

"But she's not giving testimony," the judge said. "She's explaining what she's doing so we'll be able to follow along."

"How is that different from collecting any other evidence?" Salvia said. "If she were any other expert, I would be allowed to question her methodology."

I had to give it to him, he was making a point. A point that could keep us here for hours.

"Your honor," I said, "may I ask Mr. Salvia a question?"

The judge gave me his long, considering look, then nodded. "I'll allow it."

I looked at the lawyer. He wasn't that much taller than me, but he stood straight for every inch of it. So did I, but his stance was more aggressive, as if he were squaring himself for an attack. I guess in a way he was.

I'd testified in court a few times when a lawyer got clever and tried to win an appeal on a zombie who had said this will is real, not this one. I'd even been called into court for an insurance company that decided to appeal the zombie's testimony on the grounds that the dead were not competent to give testimony. I'd stopped getting dragged into court to defend myself after I'd offered to bring the zombie into court to give open court testimony. The offer was accepted. And that was back in the days when my zombies actually looked more like the shambling dead than a person.

We'd all made the papers, and the media had made much of the fact that the mean ol' company had traumatized the family a second time. In fact, it had been the beginning of a countersuit for mental distress. The insurance company would eventually pay more in the second suit than in the original life insurance claim. Everyone learned their lesson, and I got to stay in the cemetery and out of the courtroom. But I'd spent weeks being drilled with the argument that I was not a true forensic expert. Salvia was about to hear me spit that argument back at him.

"Mr. Salvia, would you say that most evidence is open to interpretation depending on which expert you get to interpret that evidence?"

He considered that for a moment. Most lawyers won't answer questions fast, especially not in court. They want to think it through first. "I would agree with that statement."

"If I was here to collect DNA or some other physical evidence, my actions might be open to scrutiny, because my method of collection could impact how reliable my evidence was, correct?"

Micah gave me a look. I shrugged at him. I could talk lawyer-speak up to a point, in a good cause. Getting us out of here before five a.m. was a good cause.

Salvia finally answered a cautious "I would agree. Which is why I need to question your methods, so I can understand them well enough to represent my client."

"But, Mr. Salvia, what I'm about to do is not open to interpretation of any kind."

He turned to the judge. "Your honor, she is refusing to explain her methods. If I don't understand what the marshal is doing, then how will I be able to adequately defend my client?"

"Marshal Blake," the judge said, "I'm sorry that I opened this issue with my request for information, but I can see the defense's point."

"For most experts, I would see his point, too, your honor, but may I make one more point before you rule on whether the defense gets to question my every move?"

"I won't allow him to question your every move, Marshal," he said with a smile that even by moonlight seemed self-satisfied. Or maybe I was just watching the entire night go up in questions, and that was making me grumpy. I'd never had to raise the dead while being questioned by hostile lawyers. It didn't sound like a fun evening. "But I will allow you to make your point."

"If I raise Emmett Rose from the dead tonight, you'll be here to see it, right?"

"Are you speaking to me, Marshal Blake?" asked the defense lawyer.

"Yes, Mr. Salvia, I am speaking to you." I fought to keep the impatience out of my voice.

"Could you repeat the question?" he asked.

I repeated it, then added, "If I fail to raise Emmett Rose from the dead tonight, you'll be here to see that, too, right?"

I could see him frown even in the cooler darkness under the trees. "Yes." But he said it slowly, as if he didn't see the trap but suspected that there was one.

"I will either raise the zombie from this grave, or I will not. Correct, Mr. Salvia?"

"Your honor, what is Marshal Blake trying to get at?" Salvia asked.

"Do you concede that my raising Emmett Rose from the dead is either a yes or no question? Either he pops out of the grave, or he does not."

"Yes, yes, I concede that, but I still don't see—"

"Would you say that the zombie rising from the grave is open to interpretation?" I asked.

Salvia opened his mouth, closed it. "I'm not sure I understand the question."

The judge said, "Marshal Blake has made her point. Either the zombie will rise from the grave, or it won't. We will all be here to see the zombie either rise, or not rise. It isn't open to interpretation, Mr. Salvia. Either she will do what she's being paid for, or she won't. It either works or it does not."

"But the ritual she chooses to raise the dead could affect the ability of Mr. Rose to give intelligent testimony."

The judge asked me, "Is that true? Marshal, could your choice of rituals affect the zombie?"

"Not the ritual. No, your honor. But the ability of

the animator." The moment that last bit left my mouth, I flinched. I should have stopped with "No, your honor." Dammit.

"Explain the last part of that statement," the judge said.

See, I'd said too much. Given them something to question and be confused by. I knew better than that.

"The greater the degree of power the animator has, and sometimes the more practice he or she has at raising the dead, the better their zombies are."

"Better how?" he asked.

"More alive. The greater the power used, the more alive the zombie will appear. You'll also get more of their personality, more of what they were like in life."

Again, I'd overexplained. What was the matter with me tonight? The moment I thought it, I knew, or thought I knew. The dead were whispering to me. Not in voices—the true dead have no voices—but in power. It should have taken energy from me to raise a zombie. They shouldn't have been offering power up to me, like some sort of gift. Power over the dead comes with a price, always. Nothing's free with the dead.

Micah touched my arm. It startled me. I looked at him, and he said softly, "Are you all right?"

I nodded.

"The judge is talking to you."

I turned back to the judge and apologized. "I'm sorry, your honor. Could you repeat what you just said?"

He frowned at me but said, "You seemed distracted just then, Marshal Blake."

"I'm sorry, your honor. I'm just thinking about the job ahead."

"Well, we'd like you to concentrate a little harder on this part of the proceedings before you rush ahead of us."

I sighed, swallowed a half dozen witty and unhelpful things, and settled for, "Fine, what did you say that I missed?"

Micah touched my arm again, as if my tone might have been a little less than polite. He was right. I was getting angry. That old tension in my shoulders and along my arms was settling in.

"What I said, Marshal, was I was under the impression that only a blood sacrifice would give you that much life in a zombie."

I thought better of the judge. He'd done some research, but not enough. "There's always blood involved in raising the dead, your honor."

"We understand that the FBI was requested to supply you with poultry," he said.

Any normal human being would have said, *Is that what the chicken is for?* Court time is not the same as real time; it's sort of like football time. What should take five minutes will take thirty.

"Yes, that is why the chicken was requested." See, I could talk the long way 'round the mountain, too. If a question has a simple yes or no answer, then give that. Beyond yes or no questions, explain things. Don't add, don't embellish, but be thorough. Because you're going to have to talk one way or the other. I preferred to give complete answers in the beginning rather than have my explanations be made longer on cross-examination.

"How does the chicken help you with this protective circle?" he asked.

"You normally behead the chicken and use its blood, its life energy, to help put up a protective circle around the grave."

"Your honor," Salvia again, "why does Marshal Blake need a protective circle?"

Laban, our friendly neighborhood prosecutor, said, "Is my esteemed colleague going to question every step of the ritual?"

"I think I have the right on behalf of my clients to ask why she needs a protective circle. One of my objections to this entire procedure was the worry that something else could animate the corpse, and what is raised will be merely Mr. Rose's shell but with something else inside it. Some wandering spirit could—"

"Mr. Salvia," Laban said, "your fanciful worries did not convince the judge to grant your motion. Why bring it up again?"

Truthfully, one of the reasons we put up protective circles was to keep wandering spirits, as Salvia put it, from animating the corpse. Though I'm not sure spirits were what I'd worry about. There were other things, nastier things, that loved getting hold of a corpse.

They'd use it for walking-around clothes until someone made them leave it, or until they'd so damaged it that the body no longer functioned well enough to be useful. I did not say this out loud. To my knowledge, no animator had volunteered this part of the reason for the protective circle. It would open too many legal problems when we were still striving to have animation be accepted as standard practice for court cases. The circle also helped raise power, and that was the main reason for it. The whole corpse-being-highjacked thing was so rare that I actually didn't know anyone who had ever had it happen to one of their zombies. It was one of those stories that always seems to happen to the friend of your uncle's cousin, who no one actually ever met. I wasn't going to help Salvia keep us here all night.

"Mr. Laban is right," the judge said. "There is nothing in the literature about zombies being taken over by alien energy." His voice held distaste, as if Salvia had actually proposed some sort of alien possession theory.

For all I knew, he had. I guess if the prosecution's star witness can be raised from the dead to testify, then the defense is allowed to look for unusual help, too. Aliens seemed a little far-fetched, but hey, I raise the dead for a living and slay vampires. I really couldn't throw stones.

"Marshal Blake, once you have your protective circle, how much more ritual will you need?" I think the judge was tired of the delays, too. Good—me getting impatient didn't help much. But the judge getting impatient—that could be very helpful.

I thought about it and was glad he'd phrased the question the way he had. How much ritual would I need? A very different question from, *What comes next in animating the dead?* Once the circle was up, I deviated so far from normal animating ritual that it was like comparing apples to watermelons.

"Not much more, your honor."

"Can you be more exact?" he asked.

"I'll call Emmett Rose from the grave. Once he's above ground, then I'll put blood on or in his mouth, and he'll be able to answer questions very soon after that."

"Did you say you put blood on the zombie's mouth?" Salvia again.

"Yes."

"You're going to have the zombie suck on the chicken?" This from one of the agents who had been waiting with the judge.

We all looked at him, and he had the grace to look embarrassed. "Sorry."

"Not suck on the chicken, no. But I'll spread the blood across the mouth."

"Mr. Rose was a good Christian. Isn't painting him up with chicken blood a violation of his religious freedom?" Salvia said.

The judge said, "As much as I appreciate your concern over Mr. Rose's religious freedom, Mr. Salvia, I have to point out that he isn't your client, and that the dead have no rights to violate."

Of course, I had to add my two cents' worth. I just couldn't help myself. "Besides, Mr. Salvia, are you implying that you can't be a good Christian if you sacrifice a few chickens and raise a few zombies?" The anger was creeping from my shoulders and into my voice. Micah started rubbing his hand up and down my arm, as if to remind me that he was there, and my temper was, too. But his touch did help make me think. I guess sometimes I needed an "assistant" for more than sex and blood. Sometimes I just needed a keeper.

I got a few startled looks. Salvia wasn't the only one who'd assumed I wasn't Christian. I don't know why it still hurts my feelings, but it does. The judge said, "You may answer Marshal Blake's question." I was definitely not the only one sick of Salvia's bitching.

"I didn't mean to imply anything about your own religious beliefs, Marshal Blake. I apologize for assuming that you weren't Christian."

"Don't worry about it, Salvia. Lots of people assume all sorts of shit about me."

Micah whispered, "Anita." One word, but enough.

I could have used the dead as an excuse, and it might even have been true, but the real reason was I've never held my temper well. I'm better sometimes, worse others, but it never takes long for me to get tired of assholes.

Salvia was pissing me off, and the judge with his *Please explain the unexplainable, Marshal Blake* wasn't far behind in the pissing-me-off department.

"Sorry about that, your honor, but can we cut to the chase here?"

"I'm not sure what you mean by cutting to the chase, Marshal Blake."

"Emmett Rose is the recently dead. I mean he hasn't hit one year dead. It's an easy job, your honor. A little blood, a little power, and voilà, a zombie. He'll be able to answer questions. He'll be able to be cross-examined. He'll do everything you want him to be able to do. Having experienced Mr. Salvia's questioning technique, I think the cross-examination may last a long damned time. So in the interest of all of us not spending the entire bloody night in the cemetery, can I please get on with it?"

Franklin made a noise low in his throat. Fox was shaking his head. I knew I was fucking it up but I couldn't seem to stop. I wanted out of this cemetery.

I wanted away from the graves and their promise of power. I needed my circle of protection up now, not an hour from now. My head would stop echoing with half-heard whispers like words from a distant room. Or a radio station turned down low. I could almost hear the voices, almost hear the dead. I shouldn't have been able to do that. They weren't ghosts. The quiet dead are just that, quiet.

"I will remind you, Marshal, that this is still a court of law. I can hold you in contempt."

Micah turned me to him and drew me into a hug. His breath was warm against my face. "Anita, what's wrong?"

I felt movement at my back a moment before Fox asked quietly, "Are you all right, Blake?"

I leaned into Micah. His arms held me, tight and almost fierce, as if he would press me out the other side of his body. He whispered against my face, "What is wrong, Anita? What is it?"

I grabbed on to him and pressed as much of him against me as I could, so that we were plastered against each other, as close as we could get with clothes on. I buried my face against the side of his neck, drawing in the warm, sweet scent of his skin. Soap, the slight sweetness of his cologne, and underneath that the scent of his skin. The scent of Micah. And underneath that, that faint, neck-ruffling scent of leopard. The moment I smelled it, I felt better. That musky, almost-sharp scent of leopard helped chase back the almost-voices of the dead.

"Do you want me to hold you in contempt, Marshal Blake?" The judge's voice dragged me back from Micah's skin, pulled me away from falling into the warmth and life of him.

I barely turned my head to look at the judge, but it felt like some huge physical wrenching. The moment I couldn't bury my face in Micah's skin, the voices were back. The dead were trying to talk to me. They shouldn't have been doing that. Ghosts would sometimes do that if they couldn't find a medium to speak with, but once you were in a grave, you weren't supposed to be this lively.

I looked at the judge and tried to explain what was happening without giving Salvia more ammunition to delay things. "Your honor—" And I had to clear my throat to make my voice reach him only a few yards away. I tried again, pressing Micah's body against mine. Even with everything that was going wrong, I could feel his body beginning to respond to my nearness. We had that effect on each other. It didn't bring on the *ardeur* or distract me. Feeling his body respond helped me think, helped me feel alive.

"Your honor, I need my protective circle up sooner rather than later."

"Why?"

"This is another tactic to rush these proceedings," Salvia said.

"As you're trying to delay them?" Laban said. Never good when the lawyers start sniping at each other.

"Enough," the judge said, and then he looked at me. "Marshal Blake, why is it so important that you get your protective circle up?"

"The dead feel my power, your honor. They are, even now, trying to . . ." I sought a word that wouldn't be too much. If I said, *talk,* they might ask what the dead were saying, and it wasn't like that.

Micah answered for me. "The circle isn't to protect the zombie, your honor. In this case it's to protect Anita, Marshal Blake. She let her psychic shields down when we entered the cemetery, and she's being overwhelmed by the dead."

Fox said, "Shit," as if he understood more about that whole shielding thing than most people did.

"Was that wise, Marshal Blake, to let down your protection so early?"

I answered, "This is a very old cemetery, your honor. Since I replaced Marshal Kirkland at the last minute, I didn't realize how old. There is a remote chance in a place this old that there might be problems that would affect the raising. It's standard practice to drop shields and let my power search the cemetery when I'm this unfamiliar with the area." What I was saying was half-true. I was not going to admit that my shields had been ripped away by my own growing abilities.

"Search for what?" the judge asked.

"Sometimes very old cemeteries, especially those that haven't been used in a while, like this one, can become unconsecrated. It's like they need to be re-blessed before they qualify as consecrated ground again."

"And that would affect the zombie how?"

Micah's arms relaxed minutely, so that we were still holding each other but not pressed so fiercely against each other. He was right—we were going to be here awhile. I relaxed into his arms.

"Well, it could mean there were ghouls in the cemetery, and they're attracted to the freshly dead. They would have burrowed into the new grave and eaten Mr. Rose by now. There might, or might not, have been left enough of him for him to be able talk to you."

"Ghouls, really?" He started to ask something else, but I think it was only curiosity and not the case, because he shook his head and frowned. "Did you sense any ghouls?"

"No, your honor." The fact that I'd actually dropped shields more by accident than design would be our little secret. I'd told the truth about the ghouls, but they hadn't been why my power danced out over the graves.

"All very interesting, Marshal," Salvia said, "but your shields being down doesn't change that you are trying to rush these proceedings."

I turned in Micah's arms enough to give Salvia the look he deserved. He must have had bad night vision, because he didn't flinch. Franklin did, and it wasn't even directed at him.

"And what do you hope to gain by delaying things, Salvia?" I asked. "What difference does it make to your clients whether Rose rises now or two hours from now? It's still going to happen tonight."

Micah leaned his face against my ear and spoke just barely above a breath. I don't think he wanted to risk anyone else hearing. "His fear spiked. He is delaying for a reason."

I turned and breathed against his ear, "What could he hope to gain by an hour delay?"

Micah nuzzled my ear and whispered, "I don't know."

"Are we interrupting the two of you?" Laban this time.

One of the agents muttered, "Get a room."

Great, we were going to piss everyone off. If I'd been working with police that I knew, I might have told them that the shapeshifter with me knew Salvia was lying and delaying with purpose, but over-sharing with the police—any flavor—isn't always wise. Besides, Fox had no reason to believe us, and even if he did, what good would it do us? Maybe Salvia didn't like cemeteries or zombies. A lot of people didn't. Maybe he was only delaying the moment when the walking dead rose from the grave. Maybe.

"Your honor," I said, turning only enough to give them my face but keeping most of me in Micah's arms. The warmth and pulse of him helped me think. The whispers of the dead couldn't push past the life of him. He had become my shield. "Your honor, I would love it if you would stop the arguing and let me raise Mr. Rose from the dead. But if that isn't possible, can I at least put up the circle of protection? Mr. Salvia will still be able to question me, but I will not have to cling to Mr. Callahan quite so tightly."

Micah whispered, "Aww."

It made me smile, which probably didn't help convince the judge I was serious, but it made me feel better.

"What does a protective circle have to do with why you are clinging to Mr. Callahan?" the judge asked.

"It's hard to explain."

"No one here is too terribly stupid, Marshal. Try us." Maybe the judge was also getting impatient with everybody.

"The dead are crowding me. Burying myself against my assistant helps remind me of the living."

"But you are alive, Marshal. Isn't that enough?"

"Apparently not, your honor."

"I have no objection to you putting up your circle of protection, Marshal."

"I object," Salvia said.

"On what grounds?" the judge asked.

"It is only another ploy to rush these proceedings."

The judge sighed loud enough for all of us to hear it. "Mr. Salvia, I think these proceedings have been delayed enough tonight. We are all past worrying about them being rushed." He looked at the watch on his wrist, one of those timepieces with glowing hands. "It is now after three in the morning. If we do not hurry this along, dawn will get here before the marshal gets to do her job. And we will have all wasted our night for nothing." The judge looked at me. "Raise your circle, Marshal."

The bag was on the ground where Micah had dropped it when he grabbed for me. I let loose of him enough to kneel by it. The moment I wasn't pressed against him, that breathing, whispering presence was stronger. I was gaining strength from the dead, but they were also gaining something from me. I didn't understand entirely what that something was, but we needed to stop it. The circle would do that.

The only thing we needed for the circle was the machete. I pulled it out, and the moment the blade bared in the moonlight, people gasped. I guess it was a big blade, but I liked big blades.

I laid the machete on top of the gym bag and shrugged out of the suit jacket. Micah took it from me without being asked. He'd never actually helped me at a zombie raising. I realized that when I'd told the lawyers and agents what was about to happen, I'd been telling him, too. Funny, he was such a big piece of my everyday life that I had forgotten that this other big piece was something he'd never seen. Did I take Micah for granted? I hoped not.

Removing the suit jacket had left my shoulder holster and gun very naked. With normal clients I might have kept the jacket on, because guns spooked people, but the clients were the FBI—they were okay around guns. Besides, the jacket was new and I didn't want to get blood on it. I should have been cold in the autumn night, but the air was too full of magic. Since I was dealing with the dead the magic should have been cool, but tonight it was warm. Warm the way almost all other magic is warm.

Salvia said, "Do you need a gun to raise the dead?"

I guess even when working for the FBI there are still civilians to placate. I gave Salvia a look and couldn't quite make it friendly. "I'm a federal marshal and a vampire executioner, Mr. Salvia. I don't go anywhere unarmed."

I picked up the machete in my right hand and was holding out my other arm when Micah grabbed my right wrist.

I looked at him. "What are you doing?" I asked, and I couldn't keep the unhappy tone out of my voice. Keeping it from being hostile was hard enough.

He leaned in, speaking low. "Didn't we already discuss this, Anita? You're using my blood for the circle, right?"

I blinked at him. It actually took me a few seconds to understand what he meant. The fact that it took any time at all to see his logic meant that there was something going on with the dead in the ground that shouldn't have been happening. My power easing through the cemetery had done something to the graves. If I put my blood on the ground, what more would that do? But there was something in me, or at least in my magic, that wanted that deeper connection. My magic, for lack of a better word, wanted to pour my blood along the ground and bring the dead to some kind of half-life. Would it make them ghosts? Would they be zombies? Ghouls? What the hell was happening with my power lately? No answers, because there was no one living to ask. Vampires had made it standard policy to kill necromancers. Raise a zombie if you want to, talk to a few ghosts, but necromancers of legend could control all undead. Even the vamps. They feared us. But standing there with Micah's hand on my wrist, I felt the energy from the graves almost visible in the air. That energy was wanting the blood, wanting what would happen next.

Franklin's voice came strangled from the dark. "Don't do it, Blake."

I looked at him. He was rubbing his arms, as if he felt that press of power. Fox was looking at him, too. I hadn't outed Franklin, but if he wasn't careful tonight, he was going to do it himself.

"I won't do it," I said.

Franklin's eyes were too wide. The last time I'd seen him had been over the bloody remains of a serial killer's victim. Did the newly dead talk to him? Was he able to see souls, too? Maybe it wasn't me he hadn't liked in New Mexico. Maybe it was his own untrained gifts.

I turned back to Micah. "Your turn."

I saw the tension in Micah's shoulders ease. He released my wrist, and I let the machete point at the ground. He smiled. "Which arm do you want?"

I smiled and shook my head. "You're right-handed, so left. Always better to use the nondominant hand for it."

I looked back at Fox. "If you could hold the jackets for Micah?"

Fox took them from him without a word. A very cooperative man, especially for FBI. They tended to argue, or at least question more. Micah took off his own suit jacket and laid it on top of the growing pile in Fox's arms.

Micah's shirt had French cuffs, which meant he had to undo a cuff link before he could roll up his left sleeve. He put the cuff link in his pant's pocket.

"What are you doing, Marshal Blake?" the judge asked.

"I'm going to use Mr. Callahan's blood to walk the circle."

"Use his blood?" This was from Beck, the court reporter, and her voice was several octaves higher than when she'd said hello.

The judge looked at her as if she'd done something unforgivable. She apologized to him, but her fingers never stopped typing on her little machine. I think she'd actually taken down her own surprised comment.

I wondered if the dirty look from the judge got recorded, or if only out-loud sounds counted.

"My understanding is that if you were going to use the chicken, you would behead it," the judge said in his deep courtroom voice.

"That's right."

"I assume you aren't going to behead Mr. Callahan." He made it sort of light, almost joking, but I think that his prejudice was showing. I mean, if you'll raise the dead, what other evil are you capable of? Maybe even human sacrifice?

I didn't take it personally. He'd been polite about it; maybe I was just being overly sensitive. "I'll make a small cut on his arm, smear the blade with the blood, and walk the circle. I may have him walk beside me, so I can renew the blood from the wound as we move around the circle, but that's all."

The judge smiled. "I thought we should be clear, Marshal."

"Clear is good, your honor." I left it at that. The nights when I would have gotten insulted because people hinted that all animators did human sacrifice were past. People were afraid of what I did. It made them believe the worst. The price of doing business was that people thought you did awful, immoral things.

I'd cut other people before, used their blood to help me or combine with mine, but I'd never held their hand while I did it. I stood on Micah's left side and interlaced the fingers of our left hands together so that our palms touched. I stretched his arm out and laid the blade's edge against the smooth, untouched skin of his arm.

The underside of my left arm looked like Dr. Frankenstein had been at me. Micah's was smooth and perfect, untouched. I didn't want to change that.

"I'll heal," he said softly. "It's not silver."

He was right, but . . . I simply did not want to hurt him.

"Is there a problem, Marshal?" the judge asked.

"No," I said, "no problem."

"Then can we move things along? It's not getting any warmer out here."

I turned to look at him. He was huddled in his long coat. I glanced down at my own bare arms, not even a goose bump in sight. I gazed up at Micah, in his shirtsleeves. Being a shapeshifter, he wasn't really a good judge of how cold it was, or how warm. I took a moment to glance at everybody. Most of them were buttoned up, some with hands in pockets like the judge. There were only three people who had their coats open, and, even as I watched, Fox began to shrug out of his own trench coat. The other two people were Salvia and Franklin. Franklin I'd expected, but not Salvia. If he was that sensitive, it could explain his fear. Nothing like a little psychic ability to make you not want to be around a major ritual. I might raise the dead on a regular basis, but magically it's a big deal to breathe life into the dead. Even temporarily.

"Marshal Blake," the judge said, "I'll ask one more time. Is there a problem?"

I settled my gaze back on him. "You want to open a vein for me, Judge?"

He looked startled. "No, no, I do not."

"Then don't rush me when I've got someone else's arm under my blade."

Fox and Franklin both made noises. Fox seemed to be turning a laugh into a cough. Franklin was shaking his head, but not like he was unhappy with me.

The court reporter's fingers never faltered. She recorded his impatience and my angry answer. She, apparently, was going to record everything. I wondered if she'd tried to record the cough and the inarticulate noise from the agents. I should probably watch what I said, but I doubted I would. I mean, I could try, but watching what I said was usually a losing battle. Maybe I'd feel more polite after the power circle went up. Maybe.

Micah touched my face with his free hand, made me look at him. He gave me that peaceful smile. "Just do it, Anita."

I laid the blade edge against that smooth skin and whispered, "If it were done when 'tis done, 'twere well it were done quickly . . ."

He said, "Are you quoting *Macbeth*?"

"Yes." And I cut him.

CHAPTER

11

The blood looked black in the moonlight. Micah was utterly silent as his blood eased from the cut, and I moved the blade so that it could catch the heavy drip of his blood. So calm. Calm about this as he was calm about nearly everything, as if nothing could move him from the the center of himself. As I learned more of what his life had been like, I knew that this still-water calm had been hard won. My calmness was the calmness of metal, but he was water. He was the still forest pool. Throw a stone in, and once the ripples fade, it's as it was. Throw a stone at metal and it leaves a dent.

There were nights when I felt like I was covered in dings and dents. Holding Micah's hand, with his blood welling onto the cool gleam of my blade, I could feel the echo of that watery calm.

The autumn night was suddenly scented with the sweet, metallic perfume of fresh blood. Once that smell had meant work: raising the dead or a crime scene. But thanks to my ties to Jean-Claude and Richard and the wereleopards, the scent of blood meant oh-so-much more.

Then I looked up from the blood and met Micah's eyes, those pale leopard eyes, and realized that I didn't need to look all the way to St. Louis for why the blood smelled good.

His pulse began to beat against my palm like a second heartbeat. That heartbeat pushed the blood out of him faster than it should have, as if my power, or our power, called it. The cut wasn't that deep, but the blood poured over our hands in a hot wash.

"Oh, my God!" The only female voice, so that was the court reporter. Men cursed, and someone else was making sounds like he might lose his dinner. If this bothered them, then they'd never make it through the zombie part.

I let go of Micah's hand, and the moment I did, the blood flow slowed. Slowed to what it should have been. Something about our combined energies had made it flow faster, hotter. He watched me back away from him with the dripping machete. I started walking the circle, dripping his blood along the way, with my gaze still tied to his. There were no dead whispering in my head now. The night was too alive for that. I walked the circle suddenly painfully aware of how much I'd been missing in that nightscape. I could feel the wind against my skin in a way that I hadn't a second ago. There were so many scents, it was like being blind, and suddenly being given sight. Smell was something we humans didn't really use at all, not like this.

I knew there was something small and furry in the tree over the grave. Before I'd smelled only that dry autumnal scent of leaves. Now I could smell different leaves, different scents of the individual trees. I didn't know what each scent was, but I could suddenly pick out dozens of different trees, bushes. Even the ground underfoot was a wealth of scent. This wasn't even a good night for scent, too cool, but we could hunt. We could—

"Anita," Micah said, his voice abrupt and startling.

It made me stumble and brought me back to myself. It was almost like waking from a dream. It had only been recently that everyone realized that some of my new abilities, though they came through vampire marks, made me more like a lycanthrope than a vamp. A new lycanthrope that didn't always have the control you might want in public.

I was almost back to Micah. I'd nearly walked the complete circle, as if my body had gone on without me while my mind tried to cope with a thousand different kinds of sensory input. Moments like this gave me an entirely new sympathy with dogs that were nose-deaf. It wasn't that the ears didn't work but that the nose was working so much more that nothing mattered but the scent. The scent you were tracking.

What was it, where was it, could we catch it, could we eat it?

"Anita?" Micah made it a question, as if he knew what I'd been sensing. Of course, it was his sense of smell I'd been borrowing. He did know.

My heart was in my throat, my pulse singing with that rush of adrenaline. I looked down at the ground and found I was only a few blood drops away from completing the circle.

But I hadn't concentrated at all. I'd walked circles with just naked steel and my will. Was the blood enough with me on automatic pilot? There was really only one way to find out. I let the blood drip from the machete and took those last few steps. I took my last step, but it was that last drop of Micah's blood that held power like the hot breath of some great beast. That power slid over me, over him, and out into the night, as that last drop of blood fell.

It had that feel that sometimes happens in emergencies where everything slows down, and the world becomes hard edge, like everything is carved of crystal. Painfully real, and full of sharp edges.

I realized in that crystalline moment that I had never used the blood of a shapeshifter to do a power circle, and the only time I'd used the blood of a vampire, the magic had gone horribly wrong. But that vampire had died to complete the circle, and Micah was alive. Not a sacrifice, only blood, but magically there wasn't as much difference between the two as we'd all like to believe. Cut yourself and it is a small death.

It was as if the power circle were a glass and power was poured into it, held in that small space. When I'd accidentally killed a vamp, the power had just been necromancy. This was warmer—it was like drowning in bathwater. So warm, hot, alive. The air was alive with power. It crawled over my skin, burned over me, so that I cried out.

Micah's cry echoed mine.

I turned through the heavy air and watched him collapse to his knees. He'd never been inside a completed power circle. Of course, I'd never been inside a circle when this kind of power went up. It was like some hybrid between the coldness of the grave and the heat of the lycanthrope. That's what had been wrong from the moment I'd hit the cemetery. That's why the dead had seemed more active than they should have been. Yes, my necromancy was getting stronger, but it was my tie to Micah that had made the dead whisper across my skin, Micah's nearness that had made the dead seem more "alive" than they had ever been.

Now we were drowning in that living power. The air inside the circle was growing heavier, thicker, more solid, as if soon it wouldn't be air at all but something plastic and unbreathable. I had to fight to inhale, as if the air were crushing me. I fell to my knees on top of the grave and suddenly knew what to do with all that power.

I plunged my hands into the soft, turned earth, and I called Emmett Leroy Rose from the grave. I tried to shout his name, but the air was too thick. I whispered his name, the way you whisper a lover's name in the dark. But it was enough, that whisper of name.

The ground shivered underneath me like the hide of a horse when a fly lands on it. I felt Emmett below me. Felt his rotting body in its coffin, inside the metal of its burial vault. Trapped underneath more than six feet of earth, and none of it mattered. I called him, and he came.

He came to me like a swimmer rising up, up through deep, black water. He reached for me. I plunged my hands into that shifting dirt. Always before I had stood on the grave but never in it. I had never laid my bare skin into the grave while the ground was doing things that ground was never meant to do.

I knew I was touching earth, but it didn't feel like dirt. It felt warmer, more like very thick liquid, and yet that wasn't it either. It was as if the earth under my hands had become part liquid and part air, so that my hands reached impossibly down and through that solid-seeming earth until fingers brushed mine. I grabbed at those fingers the way you'd grab at a drowning victim.

Hands grasped mine with that same desperate

strength, as if they'd thought they were lost and my touch was the only solid thing in a liquid world.

I pulled my hands out of that sucking, liquid, airy earth, but something pushed as I pulled. Some power, some magic, something pushed as I pulled the zombie from the grave.

The zombie spilled upward out of the grave in a shuddering burst of dirt and energy. Some zombies crawl out, but some, most of mine lately, are just suddenly standing on the grave. This one was standing, his fingers still intertwined with mine. There was no pulse to his skin, no beat of life, but when he stared down at me, there was something in his dark eyes, something more than there should have been.

There was intelligence and a force of personality that shouldn't have been there until I put blood on his mouth. The dead do not speak without help from the living, one way or the other.

He was tall and broad, his skin the color of good, sweet chocolate. He smiled down at me in a way that no zombie should have done without first tasting blood.

I stared down at my hands still grasping his and re-alized that my hands had been covered in Micah's blood when I plunged them into the dirt. Had that done it? Had that been enough?

Voices were speaking, gasping, exclaiming, but it was all distant and less real than the dead man who held my hands. I knew he'd be very alive, because there'd been so much power. But even to me, the only thing he lacked was a pulse. Even by my standards it was good work.

"Emmett Leroy Rose, can you speak?" I asked.

Salvia interrupted me. "Marshal, this is highly ir-regular. We were not ready for you to raise Mr. Rose from the grave."

"We were ready," Laban said, "because the rest of us want to go home before dawn."

Rose's head turned slowly toward Salvia's voice, and his first words were "Arthur, is that you?"

Salvia's protests stopped in midsyllable. His eyes were wide enough to flash their whites. "Should it be able to do that? Should it recognize people?"

"Yes," I said, "sometimes they can."

Rose dropped my hands, and I let him. He moved toward Salvia's side of the circle. "Why, Arthur? Why did you order Jimmy to put the boy's body in my car?"

"I don't know what this thing's talking about. I didn't do anything. He was a pedophile. None of us knew it." But Salvia's words were a little too fast. I knew now why he'd been trying to delay the zombie-raising. Guilt.

Rose stepped forward, a little slow, a little uncertain, as if he looked more alive than he felt. "Me, a pedophile? You bastard. You knew that George's son was a fucking child molester. You knew, and you helped cover for him. You helped get him his kiddies, until he got too rough and killed that last one."

"You've done something to his mind, Marshal. He's babbling."

"No, Mr. Salvia, the dead don't lie. They tell the absolute truth as they know it."

Micah came to stand beside me, holding his wounded arm up and pressing on it. He seemed as fascinated with the walking dead man as the rest of them. He might never have seen a zombie before, but then he wasn't really seeing one now, not the kind most people call from the grave anyway.

Rose had come to the edge of the circle. "The moment you had Jimmy put the boy in my car, I was dead, Arthur. You might as well have put a bullet in me." He tried to take another step toward Salvia. The circle held, but I felt him push against it. That shouldn't have been possible. No matter how good the zombie, the circle should have been sacrosanct, inviolate. Something was wrong.

I called out, "Fox, your report said he died of natural causes."

Fox came to stand a little closer to the circle but not closer to Rose, as if he found the dead man a little unnerving. "He did. Heart attack. Not poison, or anything like that. A heart attack."

"You swear it," I said.

"I swear," he said.

"Why put Georgie's last victim in my car, Arthur?" Rose continued. "What the fuck did I ever do to you?

I had a wife and kids, and you took me away from them the moment that body went in my car."

"Oh, shit," I whispered.

"What's wrong?" Micah asked.

"He blames Salvia for his death. Not the pedophile that hurt the kid." My stomach clenched tight, and I started to pray, *Please don't let this go bad.*

Fox said, "You'd think he'd blame the guy who put the body in his car."

"He blames Salvia because that's who ordered it done," I said.

"You're scared," Micah said softly. "Why?"

I spoke to Fox, trying to keep my voice low and not attract the zombie's attention. "A murdered zombie always does one thing first and foremost: it kills its murderer. Until its murderer is dead, no one can control it. Not even me."

Fox gave me wide eyes on the other side of the circle. Franklin had moved well back from the circle, from the zombie, from me. Fox whispered, "Rose wasn't murdered. He died of a heart attack." •

"I'm not sure he sees it that way," I whispered back.

Rose screamed, "Why, Arthur!" And he tried to walk out of the circle. It gave, gave like a piece of plastic stretched tight by a pushing hand.

I yelled, "Emmett Leroy Rose, I command you to stay." But the moment I had to yell anything, I knew we were in trouble.

Rose kept trying to move forward, and the circle was no longer a wall. It was folding outward—I could feel it. I threw my will and power not into the zombie but into the circle. I yelled, "NO!" and threw that *no*, that refusal, into the circle. It helped. It was as if the circle took a breath that it had needed. But I'd never tried to do anything like this before. I didn't know how long it would hold the dead man.

The dead man turned to me and said, "Let me out."

"I can't," I said.

"He killed me."

"No, he didn't. If he'd really killed you, you'd be outside this circle right now. If you were the righteously murdered, nothing I could do would hold you."

"Righteously murdered." And he gave a laugh so

bitter that it hurt to hear it. "Righteous. No, not righteous. I took money I knew was dirty. I told myself that as long as I didn't do any of the illegal stuff, it was okay. But it wasn't. It wasn't okay." He glanced back toward the circle, but then his eyes were all for Salvia. "I may not have been a righteous man, but I did not know what Georgie was doing to those kids. I swear to God, I didn't know. And you had the body put in my car. Did you see the boy before Jimmy moved him, Arthur? Did you see what Georgie had done to him? He ripped him open. Ripped him open!"

And he hit the circle, hit it with his hands like he was trying to reach through it, and it gave. I felt it begin to tear like paper.

I screamed, "No! This circle is mine! Within the limits of this circle of power I command. *I* command, not you, and I say no, no, Emmett Leroy Rose, you shall not pass this circle."

Rose staggered back from the circle. "Let me out!"

I screamed, "No! Fox, get Salvia out of here!" Then something hit me in the arm. Hit me so hard that it spun me around. I fell to all fours. I couldn't feel my arm, but I was bleeding. I had a second to think, *Oh, I've been shot*, before Micah moved past me, standing in front of me. Standing between me and where the shot had come from. He was pointing. I heard the second bullet hit the gravestone behind me, a sharp ping of sound.

Salvia was screaming, "Don't shoot her! Don't shoot her, you idiot. The zombie is up—don't shoot her now. It won't do any good."

I crawled around the tombstone, putting it between me and the shooter. My arm worked enough to help me scramble across the ground. The feeling was even returning to it, which was good, because that meant I wasn't hurt too badly.

The downside was that I was hurt, and now my body knew it. The bullet had only grazed me, but whatever grazed me had been of a big enough caliber that I could see things in my arm that were never meant to be visible to the naked eye. I hate seeing my own muscle and ligaments. It means the shit has hit the fan, and I'm standing downwind.

Gunshots were sounding, this time going away

from us and out into the night. The FBI were return-ing fire. Good for them. I used my left hand to get my right one moving, so I could get my gun out. I wasn't as good left-handed, but it was better than nothing.

I yelled, "Micah!" With bullets flying, I wanted him with me.

But it wasn't Micah who loomed over me. Rose bent his large dark shape over me, reaching for me. I ordered him, "Don't."

"Let me out," he said.

"No," I said. I fired into him, though I knew better than anyone there that bullets wouldn't do a damn thing.

He was a zombie; they didn't feel pain. He grabbed me and lifted me off the ground as I fired point-blank into his chest. His body rocked with the impact, but that was all.

Claws blossomed through his throat a moment be-fore I realized Micah was on the zombie's back, only his hands in half-clawed form, like only the really powerful shapeshifters could do. But you can't kill the dead.

Rose smashed me down with everything that his more-than-human body had in it. I hit the gravestone. The inside of my head was suddenly filled with white starbursts, then the starbursts were crimson, and the inside of my head spilled to velvet dark, and that was all she wrote. The velvet dark, and nothing.

CHAPTER

12

I woke staring up at a white ceiling. Micah was standing by the bedside, smiling down at me. Bedside? My left arm was taped down to a little board and there were needles and tubes going into it. My right arm was bandaged like a mummy. Someone had left a florist shop in one corner near the window, complete with those silly character Mylar balloons.

"How long?" I asked, and my voice sounded funny. My throat felt like sandpaper.

"Forty-eight hours." He found one of those cups with the little bendy straws and brought it to me. The water tasted stale and metallic in a none-too-tasty sort of way, but my throat felt better.

The door opened, and a doctor, a nurse, and Nathaniel came through the door. The doctor and nurse I'd expected. I reached for Nathaniel and found that my right arm actually did work.

He gave me that wonderful smile, but it didn't reach his eyes. They looked haunted, and I knew that I'd put that particular look there. Me, getting hurt.

The doctor's name was Nelson, and the nurse was Debbie. Nurse Debbie, like she didn't have a last name, but I didn't protest. If it didn't bother her, I guess it didn't bother me.

Dr. Nelson was short and roundish, with most of his dark hair receding around a face that looked too young for either the hairline or the weight. "It's good to see you awake, Marshal." And he laughed, as if that amused him. "Sorry, but every time I say it, I keep thinking of *Gunsmoke,* my dad's favorite show."

"Glad I could be amusing," I said, and I had to clear my throat again.

Micah gave me some more water, and Nathaniel moved up on the other side of him. He touched the side of my face, and even the brush of his fingertips made me feel better.

Nurse Debbie's eyes flicked to the two men, and then her face had that pleasant professional look again.

"First, you're going to be fine," Nelson said. He had the nurse hold my arm up while he began to cut away the bandages.

"Good to hear it," I said in a voice that was beginning to sound more like me.

"Second, I have no idea why. You took a very large caliber rifle round to your right arm. There should be muscle damage, but there isn't." He slid the bandages off, handing them to the nurse to dispose of. He took my hand in his and raised my arm so I could see it. There was a slick, pink scar on the side of my arm, about an inch and a half wide at its widest. "It's been only forty-eight hours, Marshal. Care to explain how you're healing this fast?"

I gave him nice blank eyes.

He sighed and lowered my arm to the bed. He got out one of those little flashlights and began to shine it in my eyes. "Any pain?"

"No," I said.

He made me follow his fingers back and forth; he even made me look up and down. "Your head connected with a marble tombstone, so the FBI tells me. Our tests showed you had a concussion. Initially we thought your skull was cracked, and you were bleeding in places inside your head where you don't want to be bleeding." His eyes were very serious as he studied my face. "We ran a second set of tests before scheduling you for surgery, and what do you think, Marshal? No internal bleeding. Gone. We thought we'd read the first test wrong, but I've got the pictures to show what we saw that first night. There was a crack in your skull, and you were bleeding, but later that morning, it had stopped. In fact, the second set of tests shows the fracture healing. Healing like your arm is healing." His serious expression intensified.

"You know, the only person I've ever seen heal damage like this was a lycanthrope."

"Really," I said, giving him my best blank face.

"Really," he said, and looked at Micah. He had his sunglasses back on over his kitty-cat eyes, but something about the way Nelson looked at him said the doctor had probably seen Micah without the glasses. "We had to type you for surgery. There are certain things we look at it in a blood test, just routine these days. Guess what we found?"

"No idea," I said.

"Weird fucking shit," he said.

I laughed. "Should I be worried? I mean, are doctors supposed to say 'weird fucking shit' to their patients?"

He shrugged, laughed, but it was too late to go back to the nice roly-poly doctor disguise. There was a very sharp mind in there, and someone who only did good bedside manner because he was supposed to.

Nurse Debbie moved, almost uneasily, beside him.

"You're not a lycanthrope, but you're a carrier,

which is impossible. A person either has lycanthropy, or she doesn't. You're actually carrying around four different kinds. Wolf, leopard, lion, and one we can't even identify, all of which is impossible. You can't catch more than one kind of lycanthropy, because once you've got one, it makes you immune to the others." He looked at me as if the look would be enough and I'd crack and confess.

I just blinked at him. I'd suspected the leopard and wolf, but the only time I'd been touched by a were-lion had resulted in tiny wounds. They had been from Micah's old leader, Chimera, in lionman form. He'd bled me, but it was unusual to catch feline-based lycanthropy from such small damage. Lucky fucking me.

"Did you hear me, Marshal? You're carrying four different kinds of lycanthropy." He kept giving me his hard-as-nails look.

I kept blinking at him. If he thought his threatening doctor face was enough to get me talking, then he hadn't seen anything truly scary in his life. I just looked at him.

"Why do I think this isn't news to you?"

I shrugged, the tubes and needles pulling on my left arm. That hurt worse than anything else. "I got attacked by some shapeshifters a few years back, but lucky me, I didn't catch anything."

"Don't you get it, Blake? I'm telling you that you did catch it. It's floating around in your veins right now. But you aren't a lycanthrope, are you?"

I shook my head. "No."

"Why aren't you?"

I shrugged again. "Honestly, Doc, I don't know."

"Well, if we could figure out how to put this into other people and not make them shifters, we could make people pretty much indestructible."

"I'd tell you how it works if I knew."

He stared down at me with that hard look again. "Why don't I believe that?"

I smiled. "If I could tell you something that would help millions of people, I would. But I think I'm sort of a metaphysical miracle, Doc."

"I read the papers. I watch the news," he said. "I know you're the human servant of the St. Louis

Master of the City. Is that what makes this kind of healing possible?"

"I honestly don't know, Doc. Not for certain."

"Does being a vampire's human servant help you heal like this?"

"It helps me be harder to hurt," I said.

"And the lycanthropy?"

"That I can't answer, Doc."

"Can't, or won't?"

"Can't," I said.

He made an impatient sound. "Fine. You're fit, well enough to go home. I'll get the paperwork started." He moved toward the door. He turned with his hand on the door. "If you ever figure out how the healing works, I'd love to know."

"If it's something that can be duplicated, I'll share," I said.

He left shaking his head.

I looked at the nurse, and she wouldn't meet my eyes.

"I need to take out the IVs." Debbie hesitated,

then said, "A little privacy, maybe?" She said it like she wasn't certain. Why was she so nervous?

Micah and Nathaniel glanced at me. I shrugged again. Nathaniel smiled at me, and the smile had a touch of mischief in it. Micah shook his head, smiling as well, and they left.

Debbie was as gentle as she could be. It actually hurt more for the tape to come off than the needle. When she had my arm free of all the paraphernalia, she said in an almost embarrassed voice, "Which one of them is your boyfriend?"

"You mean, Micah and Nathaniel?"

"Yes," she said.

"Both of them are."

She gave me a look. "Mr. Callahan told you to say that, didn't he? They've been incorrigible, teasing all of us."

"Teasing all of you?" I made it a question.

"Saying that you lived with both of them, then trying to make us guess which of them is your boyfriend." She actually blushed. "There's a betting pool, so whichever of us was here when you first woke had to ask."

"A betting pool for what?"

"Which one is your boyfriend. Some people even bet that they both were. Some even said neither." She looked almost painfully embarrassed. "I have to ask. I'm sorry."

"I live with both of them," I said.

She gave me that look again, like she didn't believe me.

"Honest, cross my heart and hope to—well, you know."

She shook her head. "And what is Mr. Graison's job?"

I had to smile. "He's a stripper."

She put her hands on her hips and almost stamped her foot at me. "It can't all be true."

The door opened behind her. It was my men and Special Agent Fox. The nurse threw them both a look, then hurried out.

"What have you been telling the nurses while I've been lying here?"

"The nurses were just trying to be friendly at first," Micah said, "but when we answered their questions truthfully, they didn't believe us."

"No one lives with two men," Nathaniel said, mimicking someone's voice that I didn't remember hearing. "And federal marshals don't live with strippers."

"Once we knew you were going to be all right, Nathaniel teased them a little," Micah said.

Fox laughed. "A little."

I held my left hand out to Nathaniel, and he took it with a smile. "You mad?" he asked.

"No. It was the crack about federal marshals not living with strippers, wasn't it?" I said.

He shrugged. "Maybe."

"The nursing staff seemed more interested in your boyfriends than in you," Fox said.

"Well," I said, "it's hard to compete when the guys are this cute."

Micah came around and took my other hand. He ran his finger over the new scar. "You've finally got one on your right arm."

I sighed. "My only unscarred arm. Damn."

Fox said, "I come all the way down here to tell you what you missed, and I don't think you give a damn."

I smiled at Fox. "Truthfully, I'm just glad to be alive. When I hit that marble, I knew I was hurt."

His face went very serious. "Yeah, you were hurt. We all thought . . ." He waved it away. "It doesn't matter what we thought. When you went down, the zombie attacked Salvia. We couldn't stop him. Not to mention he had a shooter in the cemetery."

"I remember Salvia saying something about not shooting me now. That the zombie was up and it wouldn't help anything."

"He wasn't delaying to be irritating. He was delaying to give the new hit man time to get to the cemetery. The idea was that with you dead or badly injured, they'd have more time to think of a plan C."

"Plan C? What happened to plan A and B?"

Micah began to rub his thumb over my knuckles in small circles. Nathaniel pressed my hand against his chest. Whatever I was about to hear, I wasn't going to like it.

Fox told me, "After you and Micah went to a

different hotel, a salesman checked into the room that we'd reserved for Marshal Kirkland. The salesman was shot in his room. Then the killer put a 'Do Not Disturb' sign on the door and probably took a plane to a different country. A very clean, very professional hit. Micah wanting a romantic weekend may have saved your lives."

Micah kept stroking my hand, and Nathaniel kept holding on, as if there was more to come.

"Salvia must have gotten the shock of his life when he got word that Marshal Anita Blake was coming to raise the zombie. He scrambled around and hired a not-so-clean, not-so-professional hit."

"But it almost worked," Micah said.

"I finally remembered where I knew Salvia's name from," I said. "He's a lawyer for some old-fashioned mob, real hard-core Italian."

Fox nodded.

"If I understood what Salvia and Rose were arguing about, then Georgie is the son of the head of that family. He's a pedophile, and Salvia and others had helped cover it up."

"Yes."

"Jesus, Mary, and Joseph, Fox, didn't you think the son's family would try to stop the testimony?"

"Old-fashioned mob does not attack federal officers. It's bad for business," Fox said.

"Old-fashioned is the operative phrase here, Fox. If what's left of the Italian mob found out one of their own had hidden a violent pedophile, even his own son, the Feds would be the least of Georgie boy's family's worries. The other mobsters would clean house on their own long before subpoenas and trial dates caught up with them."

"In retrospect, you're right," he said.

"In retrospect, you could have gotten Anita killed," Micah said.

Fox took in a lot of air and let it out slow. "You're right, Micah. I almost fucked up your life again."

I frowned at them both. "What are you guys talking about now?"

"When Micah was in a bed like you are now, I told him that I had wanted to put out an alert two days before he and his uncle and cousin went hunting.

I wanted to put out an alert to keep the hunters out of the woods, but I wasn't the agent in charge. Hell, I was just the Indian who got lucky, because some of the first kills were on Indian land. I was outvoted, and I liked my career more than I liked the idea of saving lives. I told Micah that I owed him for that." Fox looked at all of us. "And now I owe him again, because we should have taken more precautions for your safety."

I looked at him. "I didn't think the FBI was allowed to admit they were wrong."

He smiled, but not like he was entirely happy. "If you tell anyone, I'll deny it."

I raised Micah's hand to my lips and kissed him. It took some of the anger out of his face. I kissed Nathaniel's hand too, and held them close. "I'm just glad to be alive, Agent Fox."

He nodded. "I'm glad, too." Then he headed for the door.

When the door closed behind him, Micah let out a breath I hadn't realized he'd been holding. "Every time I see that man, something bad happens in my life."

I tugged on his hand so he'd look at me. "What happened to the zombie?"

He gave a frown that showed even around the sunglasses. "I know Salvia tried to kill you, but you ask first about the zombie?"

"Salvia's dead," I said.

He nodded. "I thought you were unconscious by then."

"I was, but once I wasn't there to help with the zombie, it tore him apart, right?"

"Yes," he said.

"He deserved to die," Nathaniel said, and there was a look in his face, so fierce, so pitiless, that it almost scared me. I'd seen a lot of looks on his face, but never one so cold.

"They shot the zombie, they cut at him, but he tore Salvia up."

"Did they get the shooter?"

"They got him," Micah said. "He's dead, too."

"Did they get Rose's testimony?" I asked.

He lowered his glasses enough to give me the full

force of his chartreuse eyes. The look was eloquent. Nathaniel laughed.

Micah looked from one to the other of us, then finally back at me. "Do you seriously think that with you dying, Salvia dead, and an assassin gunned down, they were going to question the zombie?"

"Well, why not? They had to wait for the ambulance, right?"

Micah shook his head. Nathaniel laughed again and leaned over to plant a kiss on my forehead. He looked at Micah. "If she'd been there and awake, she'd have questioned the zombie," he said.

"Fine, if they didn't question Rose, what happened to him? Without me they couldn't put him back in the grave."

"Larry flew up."

Nathaniel pointed to the huge bunch of Mylar balloons. "Those are from Larry and Tammy."

I realized then what the death of the salesman would have meant for Larry. It wouldn't have been some salesman in the wrong place at the wrong time; it would have been Marshal Larry Kirkland dead.

"He was really upset, Anita. He blamed himself."

"Not his fault." I squeezed Micah's hand. "Though thanks for the romantic hotel room. Who knew it would be a lifesaver?"

"Let's get you dressed," he said, "and go home."

Nathaniel kissed my hand and started finding my clothes, wherever the nurses had hidden them. Micah went for the door to see if Dr. Nelson needed any help getting me signed out. He stopped in the doorway and said, "You scared the hell out of me. Don't do it again."

"I'll do my best," I said.

He leaned his forehead against the door edge for a moment, then he looked at me. "I love you."

I had a lump in my throat that hadn't been there a second before. "I love you, too."

Nathaniel was suddenly airborne. I had a second to make that little-girl *eep* sound, and then he landed around me on all fours, perfectly. "Does anything hurt?"

"No," I said, breathless and laughing.

"Good," he said, and he lay down on top of me, pressing his body against me hard enough that I had to either spread my legs for him or risk bruising tender bits on both of us. He lay above the sheets, both of us fully clothed, but he was suddenly above me, and the look in his eyes was more intimate than nakedness could have made it. Because what was in his eyes was emotion too real for lust, too real for anything but a very different four-letter word.

He kissed me. He kissed me as if my mouth were air, food, and water, and he'd been dying without the taste of it. That's when Nurse Debbie and the other members of her betting pool came in. They screamed like freshmen at their first frat party. And I'd thought nurses were jaded.

Turn the page for a sneak look at

Danse Macabre

by
Laurell K. Hamilton

Coming in June from Berkley Books

It was the middle of November. I was supposed to be out jogging, but instead I was sitting at my breakfast table talking about men, sex, werewolves, vampires, and that thing that most unmarried but sexually active women fear most of all—a missed period.

Veronica "Ronnie" Sims, best friend and private detective, sat across from me at my little four-seater breakfast table. The table sat on a raised alcove in a bay window. I did breakfast most mornings looking at the view out onto the deck and the trees beyond. Today, the view wasn't pretty, because the inside of my head was too ugly to see it. Panic will do that to you.

"You're sure you missed October? You didn't just count wrong?" Ronnie asked.

I shook my head and stared into my coffee cup. "I'm two weeks overdue."

She reached across the table and patted my hand. "Two weeks—you had me scared. Two weeks could be anything, Anita. Stress will throw you off that much, and God knows you've had enough stress." She squeezed my hand. "That last serial killer case was only about two weeks ago." She squeezed my hand harder. "What I read in the paper and saw on the news was bad."

I'd stopped telling Ronnie all my bad stuff years ago, when my cases as a legal vampire executioner had gotten so much bloodier than her cases as a private eye. Now I was a federal marshal, along with most of the other legal vamp hunters in the United States. It meant that I had even more access to even more awful shit. Things that Ronnie, or any of my female friends, didn't want to know about. I didn't

fault them. I'd rather not have had that many night-
mares in my own head. No, I didn't fault Ronnie, but
it meant that I couldn't share some of the most awful
stuff with her. I was just glad we'd made up a long-
standing grumpiness in time to have her here for this
particular disaster. I was able to talk about the bad
parts of the cases with some of the men in my life,
but I couldn't have shared the missed period with
any of them. It concerned one of them entirely too
much.

She squeezed my hand hard and leaned back. Her
gray eyes were all sympathy and apology. She was
still feeling guilty that she'd let her issues about com-
mitment and men rain all over our friendship. She'd
had a brief, disastrous marriage years before I met
her. She'd come here today to cry on my shoulder
about the fact that she was moving in with her
boyfriend, Louie Fane—Dr. Louis Fane, thank you very
much. He had his doctorate in biology and taught
at Washington University. He also turned furry once
a month and was a lieutenant of the local wererat
rodere—their word for pack.

"If Louie wasn't hiding what he was from his colleagues, we'd be going to the ballet tomorrow and the big party afterward," she said.

"He teaches people's kids, Ronnie. He can't afford to find out what they'd do if they found out he had lycanthropy."

"College isn't 'kids.' It's definitely grown-up."

"Parents won't see it that way," I said. I looked at her and finally said, "Are you changing the subject?"

"It's only two weeks, Anita, after one of the most violent cases you've ever had. I wouldn't even lose sleep over it."

"Yeah, but your period is erratic. Mine's not. I've never been two weeks late before."

She pushed a strand of blond hair back behind her ear. The new haircut framed her face nicely, but it didn't keep her hair out of her eyes, and she was always pushing it back. "Never?"

I shook my head and sipped coffee. It was cold. I got up and went to dump it in the sink.

"What's the latest you've ever been?" she asked.

"Two days. I think five once, but I wasn't having sex with anyone, so it wasn't scary. I mean, unless there was a star in the east I was safe, just late." I poured coffee from the French press, which emptied it. I was so going to need more coffee.

Ronnie came to stand next to me while I put more hot water on the stove. She leaned her butt against the cabinets and drank her coffee, but she was watching me. "Let me run this back at you. You've never been two weeks late, ever, and you've never missed a whole month before?"

"Not since this whole mess started when I was fourteen, no."

"I always envied you the regular as clockwork schedule," she said.

I started dismantling the French press, taking out the lid with its filter on a stick. "Well, the clock is broken right now."

"Shit," she said softly.

"You can say that again."

"You need a pregnancy test," she said.

"No shit." I dumped the grounds into the trash can and shook my head. "I can't go shopping for one tonight."

"Can't you make a quick stop on the way to Jean-Claude's little tête-à-tête? It's not like this is the main event."

Jean-Claude, Master Vampire of the City of St. Louis, and my sweetie, was throwing one of the biggest bashes of the year to welcome to town the first ever mostly vampire dance company. He was one of their patrons, and when you spend that much money, you apparently get to spend more to throw a party to celebrate that the money was helping the dance troupe earn rave reviews in their cross-country tour. There was going to be national and international media there. Tomorrow. It was like a Big Deal, and I, as his main squeeze, had to be on his arm, smiling and dressed up. But that was tomorrow. Tonight's little get-together was sort of a prelim to the main event. Without letting the media know, a couple of the visiting Masters of the City had snuck in early.

Jean-Claude had called them friends. Master vampires did not call other master vampires friends. Allies, partners—but not friends.

"Yeah, Ronnie, I'm riding in with Micah and Nathaniel. Even if I stop, Nathaniel will insist on going in whatever store with me or wondering why I don't let him go. I don't want any of them to know until I've got the test and it's yes or no. Maybe it is only nerves, stress, and the test will say no. Then I won't have to tell anybody."

"Where are your two handsome housemates?"

"Jogging. I was supposed to go with them, but I told them you'd called and needed me to hold your hand about moving in with Louie."

"I did," she said, and sipped her coffee. "But suddenly me being nervous about sharing space with a man for the second time in my life doesn't seem like such a big deal. Louie is nothing like the asshole I married when I was young and stupid."

"Louie sees the real you, Ronnie. He's not looking for some sort of trophy wife. He wants a partner."

"I hope you're right."

"I don't know much today, but I'm sure Louie wants a partner, not a Barbie doll."

She gave me a weak smile, then frowned.

"Thanks, but I'm supposed to be comforting you. Are you going to tell them?"

I leaned my hands against the sink and looked at her through a curtain of my long dark hair. It had gotten too long for my tastes, but Micah had made me a deal. If I cut my hair, he'd cut his, because he preferred his hair shorter, too. So my hair was fast approaching my waist for the first time since junior high, and it was really beginning to get on my nerves. Of course, today everything was getting on my nerves.

"Until I know for sure, I don't want them to know."

"Even if it's yes, Anita, you don't have to tell them. I'll close up my agency for a few days. We'll go away on a girls' retreat, and you can come back without a problem."

I pushed my hair back so I could see her clearly.

I think my face showed what I was thinking, because she said, "What?"

"Are you honestly saying that I don't tell any of them? That I just go away for a while and make sure that there's no baby to worry about?"

"It's your body," she said.

"Yeah, and I took my chances by having sex with this many men on a regular basis."

"You're on the pill," she said.

"Yeah, and if I'd wanted to be a hundred percent safe I'd have still used condoms, but I didn't. If I'm . . . pregnant, then I'll deal, but not like that."

"You can't mean you'd keep it."

I shook my head. "I'm not even sure I'm pregnant, but if I was, I couldn't not tell the father. I'm in a committed relationship with several of them. I'm not married, but we live together. We share a life. I couldn't make this kind of choice without talking to them first."

She shook her head. "No man ever wants a woman to get an abortion if they're in a relationship. They always want her barefoot and pregnant."

"That's your mother's issues talking, not yours, or at least not mine."

She looked away, wouldn't meet my eyes. "I can tell you what I'd do, and it wouldn't involve telling Louie."

I sighed and stared out the little window above the sink. A lot of things to say to that went through my head, none of them helpful. I finally settled for, "Well, it isn't you and Louie having this particular problem. It's me, and . . ."

"And who?" she said. "Who got you knocked up?"

"Thanks for putting it that way."

"I could ask 'Who's the father?' but that's just creepy. If you are pregnant then it's this little tiny, microscopic lump of cells. It's not a baby. It's not a person, not yet."

I shook my head. "We'll agree to disagree on that one."

"You're pro-choice," she said.

I nodded. "Yep, I am, but I also believe that abortion is taking a life. I agree women have the right to choose, but I also think that it's still taking a life."

"That's like saying you're pro-choice and pro-life. You can't be both."

"I'm pro-choice because I've never been a fourteen-year-old incest victim pregnant by her father, or a woman who's going to die if her pregnancy continues, or even a teenager who made a mistake or a rape victim. I want women to have choices, but I also believe that it's a life, especially once it's big enough to live outside the womb."

"Once a Catholic, always a Catholic," she said.

"Maybe, but you'd think being excommunicated would have cured me." The Pope had declared that all animators—zombie raisers—were excommunicate until they repented their evil ways and stopped doing it. What His Holiness didn't seem to grasp is that raising the dead was a psychic ability, and if we didn't raise zombies for money on a regular basis, we'd eventually raise the dead by accident. I had accidentally raised a pet as a child and a suicidal teacher in college. I'd always wondered if there had been others that never found me. Maybe some of the accidental zombies that occasionally show up are the result of someone's psychic abilities gone wrong or untrained. All I knew was that if the Pope had ever woken up as a child with his dead dog curled up in bed with him, he'd want his power controlled. Or maybe he wouldn't. Maybe he'd believe that it was evil and he'd pray it into submission. My prayers just didn't have that kind of punch to them.

"You can't mean you'd actually have this . . . thing, baby, whatever."

I sighed. "I don't know, but I do know that I could never go away, get an abortion, and never tell my boyfriends. Never tell them that one of them might have made a child with me. I just couldn't do it."

She was shaking her head so hard that her hair fell around her face, covered the upper half of it. She ran her hands through it sharply, like she was pulling on it. "I've tried to understand that you're happy living with not one but two men. I've tried to understand that you love that vampire son of a bitch, somehow. I've tried, but if you actually breed . . . actually have a baby, I just don't get that. I won't be able to understand that."

"Then don't. Then go. If you can't deal, then go."

"I didn't mean that. I meant that I can't understand why you would complicate your life this way."

"Complicate, yeah, I guess that's one way of putting it."

She crossed her arms tight over her chest. She was tall, slender and leggy, and blond. Everything I'd wanted to be as a child. She was small-chested enough that she could fold her arm over her breasts instead of under them, something I couldn't have done. But her legs went on forever in a skirt, and mine did not. Oh, well.

"Okay, then if you're going to tell them, tell Micah and Nathaniel and get a test and test yourself."

"Not until after the test. I don't want anyone to know until I know for sure."

She looked up at the ceiling, closed her eyes, and sighed. "Anita, you live with two of them. You sleep over with two more of them. You are never alone. When are you going to have time to get a test, let alone have the privacy to use it?"

"I can pick one up at work on Monday."

She stared at me. "Monday! It's Thursday. *I'd* go fucking crazy if I had to wait that long. You'll go crazy. You can't wait nearly four days."

"Maybe my period will start. Maybe by Monday I won't need it."

"Anita, you wouldn't have told me if you weren't pretty sure you needed a pregnancy test."

"When Nathaniel and Micah get back, they'll jump in the shower, then we'll get dressed up and go straight to Jean-Claude's. There won't be time tonight."

"Friday. Promise me that Friday you'll get one."

"I'll try, but . . ."

"Besides, when you start asking your lovers to use condoms, won't they figure something out?"

"Jesus," I said.

"Yeah, I heard you say if you'd used condoms, you'd be safe. Don't tell me that you're not going to want to use them for a while. Could you really have unprotected sex right now and enjoy it?"

I shook my head. "No."

"Then what are you going to tell the boys about this sudden need for condoms? Hell, Micah had a vasectomy before you even met him. He's, like, super safe."

I sighed again. "You're right. Dammit, but you are."

"So pick up the test on the way to the thing to-night."

"No, I'm not going to rain all over Jean-Claude's meeting. He's planned this for months."

"You didn't mention it to me."

"I didn't plan it, he did. The ballet isn't really my thing." Truthfully, he hadn't even told me until the masters were coming to St. Louis, but I kept that part to myself. It would only give Ronnie another reason to say that Jean-Claude was keeping secrets from me. He'd finally admitted that the Masters of the City all coming here hadn't been something he had planned, at least not from the beginning. He'd only negotiated it so the vampire dancers could cross many different vamp territories without problems. Jean-Claude agreed the meet was a good idea, but he was also nervous about it. It would be the largest gathering of Masters of the City in American history. And you don't bring that many big fish together without worrying about shark attacks.

"And how will Mr. Fang-Face feel about being a father?"

"Don't call him that."

"Sorry, how will Jean-Claude feel about being a daddy?"

"It's probably not his."

She looked at me. "You're having sex with him—a lot. Why isn't it his?"

"Because he's more than four hundred years old, and when a vampire gets that old, he isn't very fertile. That goes for Asher, and Damian, too."

"Oh, God," she said. "I'd forgotten that you had sex with Damian."

"Yeah," I said.

She covered her eyes with her hands. "I'm sorry, Anita. I'm sorry that it's weirding me out that my up-tight monogamous friend is suddenly sleeping with not one but three vampires."

"I didn't plan it that way."

"I know that." She hugged me, and I stayed stiff against her. She wasn't being comforting enough for me to relax in her arms. She hugged me tighter. "I'm sorry. I'm sorry I'm being a jerk. But if it's not the vampires, then who else but your houseboys."

I pulled away from her. "Don't call them my houseboys. They have names, and just because I like living with someone and you don't, doesn't make that my problem."

"Fine. That leaves Micah and Nathaniel."

"Micah is fixed, remember? So it can't be him."

Her eyes went wide. "That leaves Nathaniel. Jesus, Anita, Nathaniel as the father to be."

A moment ago, I might have agreed with her, but now it pissed me off. It wasn't her place to disparage my boyfriends. "What's wrong with Nathaniel?" I said, and my voice was not entirely happy.

She put her hands on her hips and gave me a look. "He's twenty and a stripper. Twenty-year-old strippers are the entertainment at your bachelorette party. You don't have babies with them."

I let the anger seep into my eyes. "Nathaniel told me you didn't see him as real, as a person. I told him he was wrong. I told him you were my friend, and you wouldn't disrespect him like that. I guess *I* was wrong."

She didn't back down or apologize. She was angry and staying that way. "Last time I checked, Nathaniel was supposed to be food, just food, not the love of your life."

"I didn't say he was the love of my life, and yeah, he started out as my *pomme de sang,* but that doesn't—"

But she interrupted me. "Your apple of blood, right? That's what *pomme de sang* means."

I nodded.

"If you were a vampire you'd be taking blood from your little stripper, but thanks to that blood-sucking son of a bitch, you have to feed off of sex. Sex, for God's sake! First that bastard made you his blood whore, and now you're just a—" She stopped abruptly, a startled, almost frightened expression on her face, as if she knew she'd gone too far.

I gave her a flat, cold look. The look that says my

anger has moved from hot to cold. It's never a good sign. "Go on, Ronnie, say it."

"I didn't mean it," she whispered.

"Yeah," I said, "you did. Now I'm just a whore." My voice sounded as cold as my eyes felt. Too angry and too hurt to be anything but cold. Hot angry can feel good, but the cold will protect you better.

She started to cry. I stared at her, speechless. What the hell was going on? We were fighting; she wasn't allowed to cry in the middle of it. Especially not when she was the one being a cruel bastard. I could count on one hand the times I'd seen Ronnie cry and still have fingers left over.

I was still angry, but I was puzzled too, and that took a little of the edge off. "Shouldn't I be the one in tears here?" I asked, because I couldn't think of what else to say. I was mad at her and I'd be damned if I would comfort her right now.

She spoke in that breathless, hiccuping voice that serious crying can give you. "I'm sorry. Oh, God, Anita, I'm sorry. I'm just so jealous."

I raised eyebrows at her. "What are you talking about? Jealous of what?"

"The men," she said in that shivering, uncertain voice. It was like she was someone else for a moment, or maybe this was a part of Ronnie that she didn't let people see. "All the damned men. I'm about to give up everybody. Everybody but Louie, and he's great, but dammit, I've had lovers. I hit triple digits."

I wasn't sure that being able to number your lovers at over a hundred was a good thing, but it was something that Ronnie and I had also agreed to disagree on a long time ago. I did not say, *Look who's the whore* or other hurtful remarks I could have made. I let all the cheap shots I could have made go. She was the one crying.

"And now I'm giving it all up, all of it, for just one man." She leaned her hands against the cabinet as if she needed the support.

"You said sex with Louie was great. I think you've used words like *fantastic,* and *mind-blowing.*"

She nodded, her hair spilling around her face so that I couldn't see her eyes for a moment. "It is, he is, but he's only one man. What if I get bored, or he gets bored with me? How can just one be enough? The last time we were both cheating a month after the wedding." She looked up at that last remark, her gray eyes wide and frightened.

I made a small helpless gesture and said, "You're asking the wrong person, Ronnie. I'd planned on monogamy. It seemed like a good idea to me."

"That's exactly what I mean." She wiped at the tears on her face in harsh, angry motions, as if the touch of them made her even more upset. "How is it that you, my girlfriend who had only three men in her entire life, ends up dating and fucking five men?"

I didn't know what to say to that, so I tried to concentrate on the hard facts. "Six men," I said.

She frowned at me, her eyes taking on that look that meant she was counting in her head. "I only count five."

"You're leaving someone out, Ronnie."

"No"—she started counting on her fingers—"Jean-Claude, Asher, Damian, Nathaniel, and Micah. That's it."

I shook my head again. "I had unprotected sex with one more man last month." I could have said it differently, but maybe if we got back to my personal disaster, we could stop talking about Ronnie's penis envy. She needed more therapy than I knew how to give lately.

She frowned harder, and then she got it. "Oh, no, no," she said.

I nodded. Happy to see from her expression that she got the full awfulness of it.

"You had sex with him just once, right?"

I shook my head no, over and over again. "Not just once."

She was looking at me so hard that I couldn't hold her gaze. Even with the tear tracks drying on her face, she was suddenly Ronnie again. Ronnie had a good hard stare. I couldn't meet it and was left looking at the cabinets. "How much more than not just once?" she asked.

I started to blush and couldn't stop it. Dammit.

"You're blushing—that's not a good sign," she said.

I stared down at the countertop, using my long hair to hide my face.

Her voice was gentler when she said, "How many times, Anita? How many times in the month you've been back together?"

"Seven," I said, still not looking up. I hated admitting it, because the number alone said louder than any words exactly how much I enjoyed being in Richard's bed.

"Seven times in a month," she said. "Wow, that's . . ."

I looked up, and the look was enough.

"Sorry, sorry, just . . ." She looked as if she wasn't sure whether she was going to laugh or be sad about it. She controlled herself and finally sounded sad when she said, "Oh, my God, Richard."

I nodded again.

"Richard." She whispered his name and looked suitably horrified. It was worth a little horror.

Richard Zeeman and I had been off again, on again for years. Mostly off. We'd been engaged briefly until

I saw him eat someone. Richard was the leader—
Ulfric—of the local werewolf pack. He was also a junior high science teacher and an all-around Boy Scout.
If Boy Scouts were six-foot-one, muscled, amazingly
handsome, with an equally amazing ability to be self-
destructive. He hated being a monster, and he hated
me for being more comfortable with the monsters
than he was. He hated a lot of things, but we'd made
up just enough to have fallen into bed in the last few
weeks. But as my Grandma Blake told me, once was
enough.

Of all the men in my life, the worst possible choice
to be the father would be Richard, because he of all of
them would try for the white picket fence and a normal life. Normal wasn't possible for me, or him, but I
knew that, and he didn't, not really, not yet. Even if I
was pregnant, even if I kept being pregnant, I wasn't
going to marry anyone. I wasn't going to change my
living arrangements. My life worked the way it was,
and Richard's idea of domestic bliss was not mine.

Ronnie gave an abrupt laugh, then swallowed it. I
was glaring at her. "Come on, Anita, I'm allowed to

be impressed that you've managed to have sex with him seven times in the space of a month. I mean, you don't even live together, and you're having more sex than some of our married friends."

I kept giving her the look that makes bad guys run for cover, but Ronnie was my friend, and it's harder to impress your friends with the scary look. They know you won't really hurt them. The fight was dying under the weight of friendship, and my problem being more immediate than her years of issues unresolved.

Ronnie touched my arm. "Oh, it wouldn't be Richard's. You're having sex with Nathaniel at least every other day."

"Sometimes twice a day," I said.

She smiled. "Well, my, my . . ." Then she waved her hand as if to keep from distracting herself. "But the odds are that it's Nathaniel's, right?"

I smiled at her. "You sound happy about that now."

She shrugged. "Well, a choice of evils, ya know."

"Thanks a lot, Ronnie."

"You know what I meant," she said.

"No, I don't think I do." I think I was ready to be angry about her thinking the men in my life were a choice of evils, but I didn't get a chance to be angry because two of the men in my life were coming through the front door.

I heard them unlocking the door before it opened, and their voices came raised and a little breathless from the run. They'd been able to run faster and farther without me along. I was, after all, still human, and they were not.

Standing between the island and the cabinets, we couldn't see the front door, only hear them laughing as they came toward the doorway to the kitchen.

"How can you do that?" Ronnie asked, voice soft.

"What?" I asked, frowning.

"You were smiling."

I looked at her.

"You smiled just at the sound of their voices, even with everything . . ."

I stopped her with a hand on her arm. One way I knew I didn't want them to find out about the maybe-baby was by overhearing a conversation. Their hearing was a little too keen to risk it. And here they came, my two live-in sweeties.

Micah was in front, looking back over his shoulder, still laughing, talking. He was my height, short, slender, and muscular in that swimmer sort of way. He had to have his suits tailored because he needed an extra small athletic cut. You didn't get that off the rack. He'd come to me tanned and stayed that way from jogging outside, mostly shirtless, all summer and autumn. He'd added a T-shirt to the short-shorts today. His hair was that deep, rich brown that some people get after starting life as very blond. His dark hair was tied back in a low ponytail that couldn't hide how curly it was, almost as curly as mine. He'd taken off his sunglasses, so when I moved into his arms I could look up into his chartreuse eyes. Yellow-green leopard eyes in his delicate face. A very bad man had forced him to stay in leopard form for so long that when he came back to human he couldn't come all the way back.

We kissed and our arms just seemed to automatically glide around each other, to press our bodies as close together as we could with clothes on. He'd affected me this way almost from the moment we had seen each other. Lust at first sight. They say it doesn't last, but we were six months and counting.

I melted against his body and kissed him fiercely, deeply. Partly it was what I always wanted to do when I saw him. Partly I was scared, and touching and being touched made me feel better. Not long ago I'd have been more discreet in front of company, but my nerves weren't good enough to pretend today.

He didn't get embarrassed, or tell me "Not in front of Ronnie" the way Richard would have done. He kissed me back with the same drowning intensity, his hands holding me like he'd never let me go. We drew back, breathless and laughing.

"Was that for my benefit?" Ronnie asked, and her voice was not happy.

I turned around, still half in Micah's arms. I looked at her angry eyes and suddenly was ready to be angry back. "Not everything is about you, Ronnie."

"Are you telling me you kiss him like that every

time he comes home?" The anger was back, and she used it. "He's been gone, what, an hour? I've seen you greet him after a day's work, and it was never like that."

"Like what?" I asked, voice sliding down. If she wanted to fight, we could fight.

"Like he was air and you couldn't breathe him in fast enough."

Micah's voice was mild, placating, trying to talk us both down. "Did we interrupt something?"

I turned to face Ronnie squarely. "I'm allowed to kiss my boyfriend the way I want to kiss him without getting your permission, Ronnie."

"Don't try to tell me you weren't rubbing my face in it just now with the show."

"Go get some therapy, Ronnie, because I am fucking tired of your issues raining all over me."

"I confided in you," she said, voice strangled with some emotion I didn't understand, "and you put on a show like that in front of me. How could you?"

"Oh, that wasn't a show," Nathaniel said from

just inside the doorway, "but if it's a show you want, we can do that, too." He glided into the kitchen on the balls of his feet, showing both the grace of his dance training and that otherworldly grace of the wereleopard. He pulled his tank top off in one smooth gesture and let it fall to the floor. I actually backed up a step before I caught myself. I hadn't realized until that moment that he was angry with Ronnie. What little cutting remarks had she been making to him that I hadn't heard? When he told me she didn't see him as real, he'd been trying to tell me more than I had heard. That I'd missed something big was there in his angry eyes.

He tore the tie from his ponytail and let his ankle-length auburn hair fall around his nearly naked body. The jogging short-shorts didn't cover that much.

I had time to say, "Nathaniel—" and he was in front of me. That otherworldly energy that all lycanthropes could give off shivered from his skin and along my body. He was five-six, just tall enough for me to have to look up to meet his eyes. His anger had turned them from lavender to the deeper color of lilacs, if flowers could burn with anger and force of personality. Nathaniel was in those eyes, and with that one look he dared me, challenged me, to turn him down.

I didn't want to turn him down. I wanted to wrap his body and that skin-crawling energy around me like a coat. Lately almost any stress seemed to feed into sex. Scared? Sex would make me feel better. Angry? Sex would calm me. Sad? Sex made me happy. Was I addicted to sex? Maybe. But Nathaniel wasn't offering actual sex. He just wanted as much attention as I'd given Micah. Seemed fair to me.

I closed the distance between us with my hands, my mouth, my body. The energy of his beast spilled around us, making me feel like I was being plunged in a warm bath that had a mild electric charge. He'd been one of the least of my leopards until a metaphysical accident had taken him from *pomme de sang* to my animal to call. I was the first human servant to gain the vampire ability to call an animal. All leopards were mine to call, but Nathaniel was my special pet. We'd both gained power from the magical bonding, but he'd gained more.

He lifted me up, using just his hands on my thighs.

Even through my jeans he made sure I knew he was happy to be pressed against my body. So happy that it forced a small sound from me.

Ronnie's voice came harsh, ugly, like she was choking on her anger. "And when the baby comes, are you going to fuck in front of it, too?"

Nathaniel froze against me. Micah's voice came from behind us. "Baby?"